The Lobby

RANDI M. SHERMAN

D1715322

WWW.RANDIMSHERMANBOOKS.COM

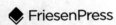 FriesenPress

Suite 300 - 990 Fort St
Victoria, BC, Canada, V8V 3K2
www.friesenpress.com

Copyright © 2016 by Randi M. Sherman
First Edition — 2016

ISBN
978-1-4602-7810-9 (Hardcover)
978-1-4602-7811-6 (Paperback)
978-1-4602-7812-3 (eBook)

1. *Fiction, Humorous*

Distributed to the trade by The Ingram Book Company

THE SHIPLEY

THE LANDMARK CHOICE OF
SAN FRANCISCO HOTELS

More than just a hotel, The Shipley is a microcosm of humanity where visitors gather, common people feel sophisticated, strangers pass as interesting, twelve dollars seems a fair price for a cup of coffee, and where our perky and attentive staff provides the gold standard in artificial concern and comfort.

Located in downtown San Francisco, The Shipley has been a celebrated destination since 1908. Admire the collection of historic clocks located in our landmark lobby which has been a popular gathering spot for generations of travelers. White marble columns, ornate balconies, and intricate woodwork transport guests back to the elegance of yesteryear. Discover the allure of the city's most charismatic and vital setting, which offers the grandeur of the past coupled with contemporary luxury and style.

Our highly polished brass and glass revolving doors are open twenty-four hours a day, welcoming guests into a timeless escape of elegant luxury and beautifully appointed rooms. People come and go and everything happens here. All stories intersect in **The Lobby**.

4:00 A.M.

The city wasn't quite awake. With the exception of the echoing electronic beeping sounds coming from dueling trash trucks and the morning shift of Starbucks baristas hustling sleepy street people away from the store entrances, there was very little activity on the streets at four o'clock in the morning. With at least two more hours until daybreak, a big, white unmarked box truck pulled up over the curb and onto the sidewalk in front of the Shipley Hotel. Even though the truck was driven slowly and carefully, its brakes squealed, then grinded to a stop. A hulk of a man, who could have been mistaken for a wrestler or "muscle" for the mob, climbed down from the cab. Face weathered, thick-necked with linebacker shoulders, hands like baseball mitts, and voice like gravel, he eyed the two bellmen who were standing outside taking a cigarette break. "Yo man, you should stop that. It'll kill ya." He let out a raspy laugh.

When he reached the back of the truck, he yanked on the lever, grabbed the nylon rope, and eased the door up as it opened. The wafting smell of fresh cut flowers filled the street.

"Get out of the truck and help me with this, would ya?" He pounded with his open hand on the side of the truck. "We've got a job ta-do. What do I pay you for, anyway?"

"Slave driver!" The cab's passenger side door opened and Benny jumped out. "Why can't we make our deliveries at a decent hour, like at eleven or eleven thirty?" He smiled and pretended to flip his hair. "Then we could do brunch. How do you expect me to find a boyfriend if my eyes look like the luggage carousel at the airport?"

"Calm yourself Betty, you'll be home by noon," Hal laughed. "Now help me unload."

The big scary man, Hal, was the florist who designed and provided grand flower arrangements for the hotel's lobby and foyers, along with cheerful boutonnières for the concierge and general manager. On odd days, Hal would just freshen up or rework the sprays of flowers, but every other day he would construct brilliant and elaborate new arrangements that dazzled every guest who passed through the lobby of the Shipley Hotel. If there wasn't a special request for a celebration, event, birthday, or wedding he could do his work and be in and out of the hotel in one to two hours—but this day was a full service day.

"Well, *Hello Dolly*, you're looking swell, dolly." Ben said it every morning as he pulled the hand-truck out of the vehicle.

The men unloaded boxes and bunches of flowers, along with vases, baskets, snippers, and watering cans. They placed everything on large rolling carts and took their goods into the hotel lobby. "Hey pal," Hal tossed the truck keys to the bellman. "Only move it if ya gotta."

Benny, Hal's assistant, was his son, who like his father, loved being a florist, but unlike his dad, absolutely hated the hours. He would tease, "Pop, why don't we just open a shop? It would be great if our hours were, oh, I dunno, like ten-ish to two-ish."

Widowed when he was thirty-eight and when Ben was just five, Hal raised his son on his own and the two were best friends.

When Ben found out that his father Hal was a hetero-sexual, he was not completely surprised. He had suspected it. There had always been little telltale signs. It was the way he looked at women, his choice in clothing, and his mannish and lumbering affect. He was apathetic about decorating, Broadway shows, table settings, and Liza Minelli. But if Ben was truthful, he'd say it was Hal's footwear that gave it away. His shoes were always sturdy and sensible. Never showing much interest in Espadrilles, or colorful Cole Haan oxfords with contrasting laces and soles, Hal actually wore his work-boots for work, not as a fashion statement. Imagine that.

At first Ben joined his father's floral business to run interference for him. Although he couldn't understand Hal's attraction to women, football pools, and car repair, Hal was his dad and Ben loved him very much. After an internal struggle and some prayer, Ben realized that if he wanted to have an unfettered relationship with his father, he would have to accept his straight lifestyle. Still, he couldn't help but worry. Hal was different, and different from the other flo-rists. Ben worried that his father would be a target for hate, ridicule, or harassment from the other floral designers. But he came to realize that his concerns were unfounded. Hal could take care of himself. He was friendly, kind, and knew everything there was to know about flowers and how to arrange them. Although he was heterosexual, his sexual ori-entation became a non-issue when the other florists realized that he was just like them. He was simply another man who loved flowers. Over time Ben found he genuinely enjoyed the floral business too, and the original reasons for joining his dad faded away.

"That's not the way it works Ben," Hal chuckled. "You know that florists have to get to the Flower Mart when the plants and flowers are fresh, around three o'clock in the morning. We have contracts with hotels and office buildings and our hours wouldn't change even if we did have a retail shop. We just don't need the headache of a lease, too."

Ben loved to watch his father work. Hal was a true artist. It was almost as if he and the flowers could communicate. After trimming and pruning and primping the arrangements, he'd whisper, "I know you're thirsty. Here you go," then he carefully added water to the vases, like he was feeding baby birds with an eyedropper.

On this day, Hal arranged the lobby centerpiece on site. The arrangement was to be placed in the center of the round, inlayed foyer table, under the other focus of the room, a baccarat chandelier. He started by placing a huge cut crystal vase—four feet tall and three feet in diameter—in the center of the table. Hal opened a box filled with the longest long-stemmed red roses available. He selected the most perfect of them then artfully clustered six or eight together into bunches, wrapping the stems with banana leaves, which created the effect of an even larger rose. Each cluster was arranged in the vase as if it were a single rose. The light danced through the water and reflected off the vase, creating a glowing effect. The flowers were perfectly arranged to allow the light from the chandelier above to shine through the array, creating a secondary bouquet of magnified rose shadows on the tile floor. The effect was dazzling—truly a showpiece.

Gina, the night shift desk clerk, walked over to where Hal was working and admired the arrangement. "Oh Hal, it's beautiful as always." She let out a little sigh. After a few seconds, she remembered something. "Oh Hal, wait a minute. The concierge, Philippe, left this special request for you." She fished around in her pocket, pulled out an envelope, and handed it to him.

Each morning after they finished their work and placed the carts, boxes, and tools back in the truck, Hal would walk back into the hotel and place a single fresh flower by the lobby boutique's rolling gate. He had only met the woman who worked there once. Her name was Pamela, and she had made an impression on him. Some days he left her a rose, other days it was a lily, or a peony, or something exotic, but he never forgot. Because his work was finished and he was long gone by the time Pamela came to work, he had never actually seen the expression on her face when she picked up the flower each day.

"Hey, Pop," Ben stood back, observing his dad carefully positioning a rose against the gate. "When are you going to ask that nice lady out?"

Hal stood up and started reading the note from Philippe. The sides of his mouth turned up. "As it so happens, I have to come back later today. Maybe I'll swing by and say hello."

"Hello? Just hello? That's it? You've been secretly romancing this woman for months. It's getting creepy." Benny raised his eyebrows. "Pop, make a move."

"Maybe I'll ask her out to dinner."

"What's this *maybe* crap?" Ben pointed at the blank envelope in his father's hand. "Write her a note and tell her what time you're coming by and that you would like to take her to dinner tonight."

The huge man blushed, "Really? I should do that?"

"If you don't, I will."

Hal reached into his back pocket and pulled out a pen. "Turn around," he said to his son. "And stand still." Hal positioned his reading glasses on the tip of his nose and held the blank envelope against his son's back. "Okay, Benny, what should I write?"

Hal read and reread the short note he had written to Pamela, then placed it next to the flower against the boutique's gate.

5:00 A.M.

Waking up next to a virtual stranger wasn't usually her style. Meredith slithered out of the bed and pulled on the skirt and blouse she had left piled in a wrinkled mess after flinging them on the floor hours before. When she heard a stirring in the bed, she frantically—yet as quietly as possible—gathered her purse and suit jacket. He, *whatshisname*, could wake up at any moment. Then what? Awkward conversation? *I never do this . . . well, except, well, this time . . . Hey, thanks for ringing my bell, baking my potato, the lust and thrust, fucking my lights out. Gotta go. Good luck with your life. I'll let myself out. Mr. Whatshisname?* She got on her hands and knees and felt around the floor and under the bed. Her shoes were nowhere to be found. Who had time to look for shoes? Although they were her favorites, she'd just have to chalk it up to a loss. Meredith squinted through the darkness as she attempted to take one more cursory glance around the room. She had other shoes in her room—they would have to do.

She slipped out of the dark room and into the hallway, closing the door ever so gently as she left, then tiptoed down the hall toward the elevators.

The last thing she remembered clearly was popping the cork on a second bottle of champagne with her boss Joselyn in the bar late in the evening. It was to toast a profitable quarter. The details were fuzzy, but Meredith had a recollection that Joselyn got a phone call and excused herself, leaving her to enjoy the rest of the champagne alone. *Think!* It was coming back to her now. There was a stranger, a young man who sat down next to her and started a conversation. "It looks like you're celebrating . . ." Meredith closed her eyes tightly, trying to remember what came next. There was a toast, some clinking of glasses, flirting, and agreeing . . . oh yes, agreeing to go with this very handsome, very young man to his room. She shook her head in embarrassment.

As she approached the elevator, she searched her purse for her room key. Blindly her hand felt around the bottom and pocket of her Kate Spade bag. Nope, not in there. When she got to the elevator alcove, she emptied her purse into a chair. The key card was not there; not in her wallet, not in any of the purse side pockets. She checked her suit jacket pockets—nope. *Oh crap*, she thought as she looked back up the hallway that she had just traveled down. It was futile. Even if she was willing to go and knock on the door and explain her predicament, she had no idea what room she had just come from. It never occurred to her to look at the number on the door. Exhaling, she pressed the elevator's down button.

Now, at 5:00 a.m., Meredith Stringer, the respected vice president of an up-and-coming company called Master Flash, found herself headed to the lobby barefoot and looking "handled." In her rush to extricate herself from the stranger's room, she hadn't had the wherewithal to look in the mirror. Were there any unsightly marks, hickeys, or stubble burn? She knew she smelled like sex. Meredith just hoped that she wouldn't be spotted by anyone she knew. She looked at her watch. *Good, it's only five.* She felt pretty safe.

Now, if only Mr. Whatshisname would just get on his plane or go to his meeting or vacation and be on his merry way, everything would be fine. No avoidance tactics, uncomfortable small talk, follow-up or backpedaling would be necessary.

She had worked so hard to rise to her position in the company, addressing rooms filled with underlings and lecturing them about focus, self-control, and pride. Now, how on earth . . . how would she explain sneaking through the lobby of the hotel, shoeless, smelling of sex, and asking for a copy of a room key at 5:00 a.m. after an unplanned rendezvous with a stranger from the bar?

Obviously, the key got misplaced somewhere. Was it in the bar? Did it drop out of her pocket when he slipped his hand up her leg and under her skirt? Was it in the elevator, had it fallen somewhere in the hallway of the fourteenth floor as they tore at each other's clothes on the way to his room? On the nightstand next to the four condom wrappers? Who knew? There was no time to figure it out. All Meredith knew was that she had to get a duplicate key from the front desk, and somehow make it up eighteen floors on the elevator and slip back into her room undetected.

What was his name? She tried to remember—was it Kirk, Ken, Chris? It was a "K" sounding name, wasn't it? He was a youngish man. From the country maybe, she tried to recall. Young, a little inexperienced but enthusiastic, that was for sure. She smiled to herself.

"Eager to please." That's how he described himself when they met. He made a point of it . . . and he proved it.

So young, probably in his early 20s, she figured, *so young and polite.* The fact that he called her ma'am, although respectful and charming, made her feel a little creepy—like an old letch, as if some investigative reporting team would jump out of the closet at any time, but oh, *all* of those orgasms. They were incredible. She blushed just thinking about it.

As she stepped off the elevator on the first floor, again she tried to remember: *What was his name again? Craig, Kirby, Connor, Kyle?*

Oh crap! Joggers! She stopped dead in her tracks, and instinctively hid behind the potted palm tree that was conveniently placed at the corner between the elevator bank and the lobby. The company's lunchtime jogging team was assembling in the lobby. That damned group of sinewy and healthful employees. They ran, jogged, pranced, floated, and unknowingly rubbed their fitness in the face of everyone who would rather spend their lunch hour actually eating. The group was clearly recognizable because they were wearing company t-shirts. There were the regular runners who were hydrating, munching a handful of nuts and stretching. And then there were the occasional exercisers, the out-of-shape folks who claim to have "played ball in college" or who consider swimming laps in the hotel pool while on vacation to be exercise. Easy to spot; they are pale and globular. The price tags that hang off of their brand-new jogging togs are a giveaway, as are their red faces and breathlessness after bending over while attempting to touch their fingertips to their shiny, clean running shoes.

Meredith's attention snapped back to the task at hand. How was she going to remain unnoticed and get to the front desk? She laughed to herself. Hers wasn't a "funny-ha-ha" laugh; it was a "what-was-I-thinking?" laugh. She didn't have to worry about having to explain her transgression to a husband, because she wasn't married. Being unattached with no encumbrances was practically a requirement when she took her job. Jump on a plane at a moment's notice? Sure. Extend a trip? No problem. Stay at the office until the wee hours of the morning? Where do I sign up? But explaining the walk of shame to coworkers? *That* would be a challenge.

What if her boss, Joselyn Rydell, saw her? Joselyn had been nothing but kind to her, but it was well known that she didn't put up with any nonsense. If someone had a calendar or a speculum, they could successfully measure that Joselyn probably hadn't had sex, a sexual thought, or even a friendship since she founded the company five years earlier. That woman couldn't have been more uptight if she was sitting naked on a block of ice. Gone were the days of letting loose, cocktail fueled and regret-filled decisions, peer pressure, loneliness, or simple horniness. There would be no excuse for questionable behavior that would be acceptable to Joselyn, and Meredith knew it.

She looked around the lobby. The joggers didn't appear to be going anywhere. Meredith had an idea. She picked up the house phone next to where she was standing.

"Front desk? Yes, well I seem to have locked myself out of my room. Yes, um . . . could you please make a duplicate and bring a key up and I'll meet you at room 1862? What? Identification? Right. Yes, you can never be too careful. Okay, I suppose my only option is to come to the desk." When she hung up the house phone and looked out into the lobby, she noticed that the running group was headed out the door and no one else who was recognizable was in sight. Meredith walked quickly to the desk.

"I seem to have misplaced my key." She tried not to blush, but she did. "My name is Meredith Stringer and my room number is 1862. May I ask you to please make a duplicate key for me?" She opened her purse and pulled out her driver's license. "See, that's me."

"Certainly, ma'am. It happens all the time." Gina smiled as she ran a new key card through the machine. "Here you go. Is there anything else I can do for you this morning?"

All in one motion, Meredith took the key card, said "No thanks" and made tracks toward the elevator bank. *Almost there*, she thought to herself. Relieved, she exhaled as she pressed the elevator call button.

When the doors opened, Meredith gasped. "Joselyn?" Joselyn, looking even more wrecked and more sexed-up than Meredith, stood staring back at her. She made a key twisting gesture with her hand and wrist. Meredith held up her newly acquired keycard, offering a pained smile as she shrugged. There is a certain etiquette that needs to be applied in a delicate situation such as this. It's a type of concordat, a silent pact, an unspoken blackmail.

Without saying a word, Joselyn held up her hand, lowered her gaze, bowed her head, and shook it slightly. It was the international sign for "I never saw you and you never saw me."

They exchanged a quick nod of agreement as Joselyn stepped out of the elevator and Meredith stepped in. She pressed the button for the eighteenth floor and waited. It seemed like it took forever, but the elevator doors finally closed.

She looked at her watch. She had a few hours until she needed to be at the conference—certainly enough time for a catnap, several cups of coffee, and to pull herself together. What *was* his name?

6:00 A.M.

Slump-shouldered and dizzy from exhaustion, Peggy stretched her neck, took a deep breath and rubbed her eyes, willing herself to be awake and perky. Dressed for the day in her high-rise, poly-blend walking shorts, a muted-colored Madras blouse, and an oversized pastel pink Jazzercise visor, she stood in the hotel lobby. It was only 6:00 a.m. Looking out through the front windows of the hotel, she could see the streets were still practically empty, and even the sun was having second thoughts about starting the day. Waking up before six o'clock in the morning was just too early, especially on a vacation.

"Hank, dear," she said sweetly, holding a Mylar-wrapped breakfast bar. "Have one of these energy grain bars. It has fiber."

He snatched it from her, peeled back the wrapper, then shoved it into his mouth and ate it in just two bites. Crumbs flying, he said, "Damned right. I'm not going to wait in line at some overpriced coffee shop for a plate of twelve-dollar eggs. We can have an early lunch." He spotted a basket of shiny red apples on the registration desk. "Mary Margaret, go get a few of those too. They will tide us over."

Peggy's movements are hindered by the beige naugahyde pocket-for-everything purse that was slung over her head and shoulder, crossing her chest. The purse strap was too short for it to be worn this way. It cut tightly between her breasts and rested at her side, just below her armpit, causing her arm to hang at a forty-five degree angle from her body.

"You can never be too careful, Mary Margaret." Hank checked the positioning of her bag. "I hear there is a lot of purse snatching going on in this city." He stood back to take a look at her. "Maybe you should put on your sweater—*you* look like a tourist. You're just inviting trouble."

It was big talk from Hank, who was dressed in brighter-than-white walking shoes with Velcro closures for efficiency, an AARP fanny pack, and his new short-sleeved sport shirt which was tucked tightly into his underwear beneath his sans-a-belt, high-water polyester dress slacks, replete with a bulging back pocket due to an overstuffed wallet.

Clutching his cartoonish city map like it was the map to the Holy Grail, Hank marched toward the morning clerk who was standing behind the front desk. He pointed at Peggy's feet. "Pick 'em up and lay 'em down. We have a lot to do today, and it's already after six."

With purpose, Hank asked the desk clerk Candice, "Is the conger . . . *conseer* here?"

Another typical tourist, Candice thought. *Ready to go at the crack of dawn. Should I tell him that with the exception of a Starbucks, nothing in this city is open before nine?*

"Good morning, sir," Candice smiled. "I see you are up early. I'm sorry sir, but Philippe, the concierge, does not get in until nine o'clock. Perhaps I can help you with something?"

"Yes, you can. We have a heavy day of sightseeing ahead of us, and I want to be efficient about it." Hank slapped the map down on the counter.

"Okay, I'll see what I can do. What would you like to do today?" Candice smiled again, as she was trained to do.

"Well," Hank began, "today we want to walk across the Golden Gate Bridge, ride on a cable car, go to the Cable Car Museum, Fisherman's Wharf, that curvy Lombardo Street, Golden Gate Park, the Legion of Honor, the Cannery, and Alcatraz."

Peggy tapped Hank on the shoulder. "And don't forget Union Square, Hank."

"You can shop at home," He called over his shoulder. Turning back to Candice, "What's the best route? I'd like to work from furthest to closest."

Hank was all about efficiency. "It's all about organization," he explained. If a household task could be wrapped up in five minutes he found a way to do it in four. "In the military . . ." Hank would say and then fill in the blank with the most Hank-a-fied, time-efficient way to do something. He meant well, but Peggy knew that he usually made it up as he went along.

Peggy had always hated being called Mary Margaret, Hun, or Marge, but Hank insisted. She endured Hank's bossy, blow-hard-headedness all for the sake of keeping him calm. They had been married for thirty-five years, and she figured it was probably her fault that he was the way he was. After all, she had been raised to be agreeable. But she secretly wanted to break free of the middle of the row, middle class, very average, superefficient life she was leading and do something wild, something unplanned. Thursday night Bingo just wasn't cutting it anymore. Anything new or different would be welcome. Dining out somewhere other than the two places in town where Hank was comfortable and where he didn't spend twenty minutes raving about the "cost of things"— that would be good. Sex with the lights on or for longer than two minutes would be a welcome change. But neither would be enough.

Peggy craved the life that she saw on the morning and afternoon talk shows. The life where people were frivolous and chatty, who drank champagne any day, for any occasion, not just at 11:55 PM on December 31st. Wearing a piece of clothing that wasn't labeled "wash-n-wear" or blended with some fabric that's name ended in -ester or -oline would be heaven after years in flammable synthetic clothing.

What Peggy really craved was some fun, something where she could shake the Aqua Net out of her conservative hairdo and throw her hands in the air. But this quick, one-night turn around trip to San Francisco would just have to suffice for now. After all, Hank reminded her, "It was a sweetheart of a deal on Groupon."

"Mary Margaret, stop daydreaming and come over here with your purse, I need my glasses."

Peggy walked toward him as she fished his Walmart "readers" from her bag. "Here you go. Hey Hank," she ventured, "is it possible to have a leisurely day? You know, take our time and enjoy each of the things we choose to do. Let's be spontaneous. Let's do something that isn't on your list." Her face lit up a little as she proposed her idea. "After all," she tried to justify, "we did spend six hours in the car yesterday."

"That would be nice, Mary Margaret, but we don't have the luxury of time here. We leave tomorrow and I don't know when we'll be back to Frisco." He turned back to his map and Candice who bristled. She, like all other San Franciscans, hated it when someone referred to their city as "Frisco."

"Well sir, yours is quite an itinerary for one day." She smiled.

"Can we walk?"

"Well sir, Mister . . . ah?" Candice was hoping to make a connection, if for no other reason than to help out his poor wife who looked to be dreading the day ahead of her.

"Ah, Mumser. The name is Mumser."

"Yes. Well, Mister Mumser. You have listed a lot of things. How long did you say you'll be in town?"

"We leave tomorrow." He didn't see an issue. "Can we walk it or not? I read that Frisco is only seven miles wide."

"Yes sir, but *this* is San Francisco. Seven miles here is not the same as other towns. There are a lot of hills here, very steep hills throughout the city. May I suggest taking a car, or taxi, or our wonderful rapid transit system?"

He ignored the suggestion. "A little exercise won't kill us. We have sturdy shoes and a map, just like in the military. Do you think soldiers complain about a few hills?"

"I suppose not, sir. Good for you." Candice placated him as she glanced at Peggy standing there behind her husband. She looked weary already, and it was just past six in the morning.

"Well then," Candice unfolded Hank's map and began tracing a route. "I would suggest that you start in the most western part of the city, near the ocean. Go through Golden Gate Park, come back to walk the Golden Gate Bridge, then to Fisherman's Wharf area where you can go to Ghiardelli Square and the Cannery. Get the boat to Alcatraz for the tour, and then when you get back . . ." Even she was exhausted as she explained the route. "You can board a cable car, heading back toward the hotel and hop off at the Cable Car Museum on the way."

Candice offered one more thing. "It's early. So I can offer up our sedan to take you to your first destination? No charge." She added. "I can have our driver take you to see Lombard Street on your way. That way you will have covered everything on your list."

Peggy had drifted over to the sightseeing brochure rack. It was filled with glossy and colorful brochures depicting smiling folks drinking wine, taking pedicab rides, crossing the bay on catamarans, and dining at restaurants overlooking the bay. Not one brochure pictured a middle-aged couple exhausted, gritty, and sweating as they hoofed it across the city in an Ironman competition style of speed touring.

Peggy walked back toward Hank with a handful of sight-seeing pamphlets fanned out like a deck of cards. "How about one of these activities? Pick one. I'd be happy doing any of them."

"Go and put those back in the rack, Mary Margaret," he reprimanded her, as if she was a child.

Maybe she was just tired from lack of sleep, or maybe she was tired of being disregarded, but Peggy began to seethe. All at once she became angry about Hank, his plans, the trip . . . her entire life. Standing there in the hotel lobby, after requesting to do something, anything that would make *her* happy, she was denied again. For the past three decades her opinion and desires had been overruled by Hank. *Today* was going to be a new and different day. She was determined. A simple pedicab ride wouldn't change the course of history or upset the axis of the earth.

She clutched her handful of brochures and planted her feet next to where Hank was standing and studying his map. "Hank, I don't want to go on a death march through San Francisco. I want to have a nice, easy, enjoyable day."

"What are you talking about? It will be enjoyable."

"For you! But not for me!" She tried to keep her voice down. "I want to go to a museum and go for a nice lunch and . . ."

Hank looked angry. "And what, Mary Margaret?"

"And . . . I don't know." She became flustered. "But that's the point. I want a leisurely vacation, if only for one day."

"A vacation from what? You don't work. You live like a queen."

Bastard. "I don't see Queen Elizabeth washing your underwear," she snapped at him. "I need a break too, Hank."

With her head down, Candice silently cheered Peggy on.

Hank did not like this side of his wife. "Fine then, go ahead." He waved his hand at her. "Go ahead. Do whatever you want to do. I'm going on the tour I've been planning. You go and have your 'leisurely day.'" He was sarcastic and condescending—plus he added those insipid finger quotes that only irritated Peggy more. "But I don't want to hear any complaints about missing out on the clam chowder in a bread bowl."

"Fine," Peggy said as she untangled herself from her purse strap and placed the brochures inside. "I'm going to start my day by going back to bed until a reasonable hour. Then I'll have a wonderful day on my own."

Peggy started to walk toward the elevator bank. But after just a few steps she stopped herself and slowly turned around. Candice was embarrassed for her, silently willing Peggy to turn around and continue to the elevators. *Go, Mary Margaret, you can do it.*

"Are you coming back to your senses now, Mary Margaret?" Hank was pleased with himself and the way he managed his wife and the situation. "Did you get it out of your system? Because I have a lot planned for the day and I really don't need to deal with your lady problems. You know how you get. Now come over here and see what I have mapped out."

Mary Margaret reached into her purse and stepped toward Hank. "Here," she said holding out a purple box. "Don't forget to take your Prilosec, and . . ." she reached into her bag again and handed him a squeeze bottle. "Be sure to put on your sunscreen. I don't want to hear about your sunburn for the next week." Then she turned around and started walking toward the elevators again.

"Where are you going now?"

"Not *now* Hank, *still*. Like I said, I'm going back to bed, then I'll be doing something that I rarely get to do—spending the day doing what interests me. I'll see you later."

A devout last-worder, Hank called after his wife, "Fine, Mary Margaret. Go ahead, but you'll be missing out on a well-planned and educational walking tour. I expect to see you back here at five o'clock, in time for dinner."

7:00 A.M.

Every weekday morning, like the walk of the living dead, business travelers make their way down to the lobby to help themselves to a complimentary cup of morning coffee from the oversized, silver plated, highly ornate baroque-style carafe which is set out as an amenity for hotel guests. Whether it's because the coffee is free, or because forty-five minutes is just too long to wait for the delivery of an eight dollar pot of lukewarm, transparent, brown water from room service, the lobby coffee ritual may be the day's only opportunity for guests to make contact with another person who truly understands the loneliness of business travel. Coffee is coffee, but 7:00 a.m. lobby coffee offers a business traveler hope and possibility. Who knows? Perhaps during a divine moment of serendipity, there might be a meeting, a kind word, or just a smile that could change someone's day or someone's life.

Without the desire or time to stand around at an airport luggage carousel, every business traveler knows using a small carry-on or overnight bag with only the essentials is the only way to go. With no extra space in the bag for casual or lounging attire, the morning lobby dwellers are dressed in either yesterday's wrinkled clothes, a pair of lightweight exercise shorts and dress shoes, or they are perky early risers, fresh and sparkly in a pressed shirt and suit. Whoever they are, they all make their way toward the shiny silver carafe at the far end of the lobby.

Road-weary Marian Bradbury, a software sales account manager, is one of the morning guests. After a half-hearted cardio workout in the hotel's gym, Marian knew she had just enough time to pour herself a cup of coffee and head back to her room for a shower and to pull on her outdated and overused power suit before driving her rented sub-compact car to a client meeting. Her pre-coffee mind sputtered as she tried to think of the perfect hook to convince the client, GroceryTron, to finally make the commitment and buy the two million dollar software and maintenance package she's selling—the whole kit-and-caboodle. Marian had been working on this client for six months. Although she felt differently, she pretended to enjoy her clients, inquiring about their children, smiling as she listened to them drone on about their lives, and treating them to expensive meals while she romanced them for business. It's what she referred to as "honeymooning." As soon as contracts are signed, the honeymoon is over and she will move onto her next *objet de l'affection*. It's a cold world. It's all about dollars and cents. Gone are the days of cultivating relationships and life-long friends through business.

This will be her third face-to-face meeting with GroceryTron in the past six weeks, the seventh in the past six months. Marian knows it is probably a lost cause. Her once optimistic and focused demeanor has faded. She has lost her touch. Her bag of tricks, sales-panache, charm, youth, and appeal have proven to be perishable like old milk, past its shelf life and no longer suitable for sale. At this moment, standing at the coffee service table, she feels like Shelley Levene, the character in David Mamet's play *Glengarry Glen Ross*. The dialogue "coffee is for closers only" haunts her. She knows that today is her last chance; the only way to meet her sales quota and secure a bonus is to make the GroceryTron deal happen . . . today.

Staring at the hot brown liquid in her cup, another movie line pops into her head, this one belonging to Annette Bening's character, Carolyn Burnham, in *American Beauty*. A determined real estate saleswoman, she repeats her mantra, "I will sell this house today." Marian chuckles to herself—she has become a caricature, the movie version of an ineffective sales person.

"Did you have a good workout?" a young man asked as he smiles broadly. He had perfectly coiffed and gelled hair, pointy leather lace-up shoes, and was wearing a shiny, slim-fitted suit. He looked slick—too slick. Not like a business-man, but slicker, like a player, a schmoozer, like someone who leafs through too many *GQ* or *Esquire* magazines to deter-mine what all the businessmen are wearing these days. He reminded her of a pocket square: just for show, not for blow.

Marian hardly heard him and decided to ignore the question.

"Are you here for business or pleasure?" He tried again, louder this time.

"Oh," Marian acknowledged that he was talking to her. "Yes, I'm sorry. I'm thinking about my day. I'm here for business."

"Me too," he beamed. "I'm here for the Master Flash national company meeting. I'll bet you are, too. The hotel is filled with us."

"No. I'm not. I have a meeting with a client." She smiled politely and continued tapping a packet of artificial sweet-ener into her cup. Sizing him up out of the corner of her eye, she could tell that he is about twenty-one or twenty-two years old. *My suitcase is older than he is.* She smirked. His suit screamed "this is my first job," and his presence in the lobby, fully dressed for a meeting that doesn't start for another hour or two, told her that this is his first professional business trip. *He'll get over it,* she smiled to herself.

"I'm Curtis, Curt for short." The young man introduced himself and held out his hand.

Surprised and a little irritated that he didn't get the hint, she juggled her cup and saucer and placed her stir stick between her teeth so she could grasp his outstretched hand. "Marian. Marian Bradbury." The stir stick fell to the floor.

"So now it makes sense." He continued, "That's why I didn't see you at the 'Welcome' cocktail party last night." He points his two index fingers at her and fired his finger pistols. "Because you weren't there. Too bad. 'Cuz the booze was free, and I got wrecked."

Marian nodded and offered a barely tolerant—yet still polite—smile as she searches for a napkin.

"So, what do you do, Marian Bradbury? What kind of business are you in?" He stood back, settling in for a conversation.

Marian's first thought was to excuse herself and get away from Curt the chatterbox, but she figures that he is just one of those friendless travelers, dying to make a connection.

After nearly thirty years of schlepping around the country, away from her home, never owning a pet or a plant and forfeiting any meaningful friendships because of her schedule, Marian knows only too well that there is nothing glamorous about business travel. Sure, when you're starting out the idea of jetting off to this or that location and stocking up on the frequent flier miles seems exciting, but she knows from personal experience that it can be a lonely business. She looked at her watch and figured she could spare a few minutes to chat.

"I'm in software sales." She sipped her coffee; it tasted awful. "What do you do?"

"What a coincidence. I'm in sales too. Well," he blushed, "currently I'm the assistant associate to the top sales associate at our company. His name is Terrace, but he goes by Tripp. I'm currently helping him out, working the phones, and securing leads for him. You know, setting the ground work." Curt added, "Did you know this company is run by women? Tripp and I can't believe how hard we have to work to be noticed."

When Marian offered an uninterested "Yup, times are changing," he continued. "Tripp says that this national meeting is our opportunity to make our presence known and let the boss-ladies know what we can do for them."

"Oh. What kind of company is Master Flash?"

Curt took a moment to size up Marian. She was attractive enough, sort of old for his taste, and since she didn't work for Master Flash, she wasn't someone he needed to impress or flatter. "It's gaming. Do you know what that is?"

She was amused by his smarty-pants arrogance. "I think so. Have you been with your company very long?"

"Not really, just a few months." He seemed proud. "As a matter of fact, I'm the only assistant associate that was invited to this meeting."

"Well, Curt, make the most of it." She offered artificial encouragement.

"I intend to. I will do whatever it takes to get ahead. I am eager to please, Miss Bradbury. Open to *all* opportunities." He leaned in and repeats, almost as if it is his private mantra, "Yes, ma'am, I am eager to please. By the time this meeting is over, I will be writing my own ticket at Master Flash."

Another eager beaver, she thought to herself. *Get in line, buddy*. At the beginning of her career, like most new professionals, she too thought the meetings held great networking and career-building possibilities. But after thirty years in the trenches, Marian knows all too well that "off-site" meetings are always a colossal waste of time. They are just an annual opportunity for the company executives to thump their chests, enjoy a couple rounds of back-slapping, golf, and cocktails, and stay in lavish suites, while the exhausted mid- and low-level employees are expected to feel special and be grateful for weak coffee, forced socializing, sterno-heated ziti macaroni and sharing a hotel room with a coworker, a virtual stranger.

Based on their short conversation, Marian knows that Curt is like most new professionals—those who think they are making an impression by being overly animated "can-doers." They ended up leaving all of their good and common sense at the bottom of an empty cocktail glass, behaving as if they were either just released from prison, or as if stupid behavior was part of the meeting's itinerary.

He doesn't know what he's in for. Marian almost felt sorry for him. She knows the meeting agenda like the back of her hand.

Each conference day begins with the eight o'clock coffee and mandatory Meet & Greet. This is an ungodly hour when and where overly tired, jet-lagged, and hung-over colleagues gather to perform the first task. They must appear adept and chipper while juggling laptops, handouts, business cards, and a full coffee cup (*with* a saucer) while also keeping a very hard, very round and rolling roll from falling to its death off yet another plate. This is the time designated for confer-ence attendees to claim the stackable chair location he/she finds more desirable for the day's presentations. Whether the selected chair is located in the front of the room, where the most anxious, Kool-Aid guzzling employees position them-selves for maximum mindless head-nodding and brown-nosing opportunities, or in the back where the more sea-soned and hung-over attendees hide, most people think seat selection makes a difference. It does not. After thirty years of corporate meetings, Marian knew the three basic rules: One, sit where no one can see your eyelids droop. Two, wear a coat, because the room temperature will be set to thirty below zero, and three, the seats closest to the door—closest to the bathroom, closest to fresh air, closest to freedom—are optimal.

At 9:00 a.m., the uninspiring, self-important keynote speaker steps onto the dais. He is usually some barely-known motivational speaker or the author of a book on the newest productivity trend. More than likely, he knows nothing about your company's business and will attempt to motivate the employees using unrelatable anecdotes, catchphrases, and buzz words and tell jokes so outdated that they could have been written for Vaudeville. He'll refer to the president of the company and speak as if they are old friends. Thankfully, after about five minutes, all the audience hears is the voice of Charlie Brown's teacher.

The quick fifteen-minute morning break begins at 10:00 a.m. "And I mean fifteen minutes, people," the secretary will shout while tapping her watch in a truly slap-worthy manner.

At 10:15 a.m. it's time for the Company President to give his "State of the Business" speech. A roomful of shivering employees are held hostage as they listen to the stranger wearing a thousand-dollar suit who is standing in the front of the room. "I want to personally thank each and every one of you for your hard work," he'll say. "Give yourself a round of applause." Like four hundred Stockholm syndrome survivors, the audience attempts to please the man in charge and begins clapping. He'll speak in general terms about the company and congratulate "the guys at corporate" for their exhaustive strategizing and work-well-done and then switch to a serious tone. "We all need to *tighten-our-belts* and *work smarter*. If not," he'll say, "I'm afraid we will all have to forgo salary increases this year." Never mentioning that the belt-tightening does not effect his private jet and pending two-hundred-fifty thousand dollar bonus.

11:00 a.m. begins the one-hour morning breakout session. This is where groups are designated for brainstorming, idea exchanging, and free-associating all while being prompted—no, directed—no, *guarded*—by Nazi-esque middle management. The biggest ass-kissers will line up to awkwardly shake the hand of a top executive, point at their "Hello My Name Is" tag, introduce themselves, and thank him or her for the opportunity to be enslaved at a company that overlooks their skills and renders them unemployable elsewhere.

12:00 p.m.: Deli platters! The executive secretary thought it would be "fun" for four hundred employees to line up to construct their own lunches in one hour. Platters of Salmonella, E.coli, and Botulism are laid out with a choice of white, wheat, rye, or Dutch crunch rolls, green salad, milky coleslaw, and very yellow potato salad. It's a great opportunity to drop names, exaggerate about how vital your position is to the company, and then scope out a possible fuck for the evening. The seasoned conference attendee will forgo the buffet and sneak up to his room for a fortifying drink from the minibar.

1:00–3:00 p.m. is designated for the degrading "team building" exercises, requiring adult professionals in business suits to play games on the filthy carpeting of the hotel's grand ballroom.

3:00–5:00 p.m.: It's time for the afternoon breakout sessions. Groups of eight to ten people form a circle of chairs and listen to one or two "managers" tow the party line. They drone on about whatever subject matter they feel they are expert in, asking open-ended questions to a group of disinterested attendees. The three-to-five o'clock session lasts approximately twenty-two hours.

5:00–6:00 p.m.: Cocktail Hour is a timed activity where participants drink as much free alcohol as quickly as possible in a one-hour period. The goal is to begin the process of losing inhibitions, slurring, and making inappropriate comments until they become sick, embarrassed, and/or offended.

6:00–8:00 p.m.: Each employee will once again be required to stand like a dolt holding an empty plate in a two-mile line at another buffet table. The fare offered is runny fettuccini Alfredo and overcooked, over-rosemary'ed chicken bathed in a pan filled with salt and condensation. Looking further down the buffet one can see grey green beans and wilted salad with granite-textured croutons and a plate of enormous cookies. Some know-it-all who had once visited "the wine country" will educate the folks at the round twelve-top table with his knowledge of the yesterday-vintage of reds and whites. Before long, the dinner speeches begin. Fortunately, the guest speaker's words of wisdom are drowned out by the clinking of tableware and din of shallow conversation.

8:00 p.m.–1:00 a.m. is identified as free time—a.k.a., more mandatory fun. Participants are encouraged to order crudely named cocktails. After a few sips, spouses, mortgages, and minivan payments disappear. With the alcohol flowing, coats, shoes, ties, and pantyhose are removed. Ill-advised as it is, beer-bellied men and menopausal women hit the dance floor. The Electric Slide, Chicken Dance, and Moonwalk are reprised as coworkers exhume their bitchin' acrobatic Solid Gold Dancer moves. Vodka induced thoughts of *I've never lost it!* keep them going. As the evening wears on, phrases like "I love you, man" and "don't tell my wife, but . . ." are thrown around. This is the last off-ramp on the highway to infidelity and career-ending behavior.

"Miss Bradbury, are you okay?" Curt noticed that Marian had been lost in her own thoughts.

"Oh Curt, I'm sorry. I guess I'm a little tired." She tried to recover, "It sounds like you have a plan in mind. Just . . ." she offered unsolicited advice. "Just—don't be too eager. People don't always know what they need . . . ."

"That's what Tripp says," he shook his head. "It's about being discreet." He continued, "Tripp was telling me that his dad has had his own plumbing business for twenty years and he says that the women who run Master Flash are like all of his female clients. He says that what women think they want might be very different from what they *really* need. So I need to be prepared to give it to them. And I'm pretty sure that I have the right equipment." Curt winked and smiled slightly. "Tripp should know. He said his dad has been servicing housewives with his plumbing for years. He always gets 'repeat business,' if you understand what I'm saying."

Did he just imply what she thought he implied? He was only talking about business—if his business was servicing female executives. Marian's first impression was correct. He is slick, too slick. "Your friend Tripp seems like a real piece of work. Can I offer one piece of advice, Curt?" she said. "You might want to work on your subtlety and dial back the misogyny."

"It's been working so far. Why are you so shocked, Miss Bradbury? Tripp says that women have been doing it for years." He looked at his watch, "Well Miss Bradbury, if I want to get a good seat and be noticed, I'd better get in there early. Good luck with your meeting."

Marian shook her head as she watched Curt walk away. *Tomorrow,* she thought, *I'll just order room service.*

8:00 A.M.

Although Florentine Moretti was a regularly overlooked, overworked, and underappreciated administrative assistant, she took her job very seriously. Without an event planner, the Master Flash executives gave some of the conference coordination duties to her. She was tasked with the ordering of refreshments and the coordination of meals, but more immediately, her job of herding the conference attendees to and from one event to another was at hand. Florentine was frantic. Yesterday's kick off and cocktail greeting went smoothly enough. But today the rubber hit the road, so to speak. Name tags, agenda distribution, and moving the staff into the Grand Ballroom for the continental breakfast buffet was afoot. Suddenly she felt the entire conference's success was on her shoulders. Annoying as Florentine was, Joselyn Rydell, the company's president, recognized her efforts. "They just don't make 'em like Florentine anymore," she laughed. "I hope she doesn't blow a gasket directing traffic around the buffet table."

"Hi, Flo," Curt said as he strutted into the conference room. Florentine blushed. All of the secretaries and executive assistants lusted after him. She shook the thought of him out of her mind. She had things to do.

Marian Bradbury was just one of the synchronized laptop roller-bag team as they moved in step from the elevators, through the lobby in coordinated formations. Some of the group branched off to the right to execute the front desk key drop-off while others continued forward through the rotating doors to perform yet another group split; half of them queued up in the taxi cab lineup while the other half performed the combination of an impatient valet ticket wave and wrist watch tap.

From the direction of the ladies' room, Natalie Guilfoyle ran through the lobby with only her purse in hand. One of her medium-heeled pumps kicked off as she ran. Stopping to pick it up, she lost precious seconds. She hit the rotating door at full speed and managed to move through without incident. Once outside, she waved her hands above her head as she tried unsuccessfully to flag down a mid-sized sedan as it pulled away from the curb.

Laughing to herself Natalie re-entered the lobby, this time taking her time. Shoe in hand, she limped toward the lobby sofa.

"Did you miss your ride?" a man in a business suit asked without lowering his morning newspaper. His question had a slight laugh to it.

"Yup," she said as she plopped down on a chair next to the sofa and stretched her arms over her head, inhaling and exhaling with a big, wide smile. "My team left me behind. I can't believe it. Well," she chuckled, "maybe I can."

"I'm sure the valet can call a cab for you," suggested the voice from behind the newspaper.

"It's no use. I don't have the client's address." She exhaled with a laugh. "Oh well."

"Why don't you call someone on your team and have them come back to get you?" He asked.

"I would, but apparently my coworkers loaded my computer bag into the car with them. My phone is in it." She shrugged. "That's just one of the problems with depending on your phone for everything. All of their numbers are programmed into it. I never bothered memorizing any of them . . . I got nothin'."

Minutes earlier he had watched her dash across the lobby, through the doors, and then try half-heartedly to flag down a car that she knew was never going to stop. Then he was tickled as this adorable woman came hobbling back in and sat down next to him. There was something about her that intrigued him. He folded down the corner of his newspaper and looked at her as he spoke. "You don't seem too upset about it."

"What have I got to be upset about? I'm happy, healthy, and now it appears that I have a free day in San Francisco, and . . ." She couldn't finish her sentence. She was struck silent by the handsome face smiling at her.

He folded his paper and uncrossed his legs. "Aren't your coworkers counting on you for their meeting?"

"I think they'll be fine. We did a lot of prep work. I think they're ready." She looked at her fingernails. Maybe she'd get a manicure.

"It sounds like you're their boss. Wait . . . do they work for you?" He put down his newspaper. "Did you plan this?"

"You can't prove it." She grinned, "And I'd deny it anyway."

"I like your style." He scooted forward and extended his hand. "My name is Patrick Montgomery."

"Well, Mr. Montgomery, it's nice to meet you. I'm Natalie Guilfoyle." She shook his hand. "Now my biggest problem is 'what am I going to do with this beautiful day?'"

"Well, we can start with coffee." He smiled and his eyes twinkled.

"What?" He had caught her off-guard. She did have to admit that Mr. Montgomery was one fine-looking and charming man, and his smile . . . oh my, it was sexy. But, "What's this *we* business?"

"My breakfast meeting was canceled," he explained, "and I could use some coffee. It looks like your dance card has suddenly opened up, so how about joining me?" He flagged down a passing bellman, pantomimed drinking coffee, and then held up two fingers.

It wasn't something that happened often, but Natalie Guilfoyle was practically speechless. "I . . . uh, I guess I could have some coffee."

"Maybe I can give you some tips about where to go on . . . on this 'beautiful day.'" He looked out the front windows. "It *is* a beautiful day, isn't it? Maybe I should enjoy it too." He pulled his phone out of his pocket and typed a quick text message. "There." He pressed the "send" button then turned off his phone and put it back in his pocket. "You, Miss Guilfoyle, are a bad influence. Coffee first, then . . ."

"Are you inviting yourself on my day? Mr. Montgomery, you are presumptuous. I don't know you at all." She was being coy. "What if you're one of those evil-doers?"

He raised his eyebrow playfully. "Maybe I am and maybe I'm not. Besides, I could say the same thing about you. You could be a vixen and are enticing me into a trap, from which I may never escape." He playfully furrowed his eyebrows then smiled. "But, I'm willing to risk it. I'll tell you what, you give me something of yours."

"What?"

He reached in his pocket, pulled out his wallet, and then handed it to her. "You hold this, for insurance," he said. "We'll only go to very public places and you can leave me at any time. But," he smiled, "you'll have to give my wallet back to me. Now you have to give me something of yours to hold."

She hesitated taking his wallet. "But I don't know anything about you." However, there was no doubt that Patrick Montgomery was charismatic, tall, and handsome, dressed impeccably and he smelled good too, but . . . Ted Bundy, the serial killer, had been described the same way. Her initial reaction was to say "No, absolutely not!" He was a stranger, after all. The news was filled with awful stories about abductions and abuse. Only irresponsible women or slasher movie actors would make such terrible decisions to put themselves in harm's way. She sized him up out of the corner of her eye. He saw what she was doing. He *looked* normal.

"What do you need to know? I'm forty years old, educated at Yale. I'm single," he showed her his ring finger, "never married. I don't have any children, I am a vice president at Commerce Bank and I have a free day ahead of me." He stood up, took off his suit jacket, then removed his tie and rolled up the sleeves of his dress shirt. "C'mon, Natalie, take a risk with me. I promise to bring you back here after our day together. How about it? Let's be two strangers enjoying a beautiful day together." He and held his hand out to help her up. "Nothing more, nothing less."

What if this is it? She asked herself. *What if this is that moment? What if he, Patrick Montgomery, this man standing in front of me, is my soulmate?* Should she allow fears and society's paranoia really jade her? Natalie wondered how many other opportunities had she allowed to pass her by? *Should I have taken that year off to travel through Europe? What about bungee jumping or parachuting? Should I have bet it all on red?* At that moment, she asked herself, *Am I going to say "no" forever?*

"Okay! Why not?" She took his wallet and placed it in her purse. "Here, you can have this to hold," she said as she offered him her hand. "C'mon, stranger—let's go."

9:00 A.M.

"Hey, buddy," a tall handsome woman with a sensible haircut and leather fanny pack addressed Phillipe, the concierge. She was waving an empty courtesy cup at him. "What does a girl have to do for a cup of coffee this morning?"

"I believe the catering staff will be bringing out a carafe of fresh coffee any minute, ma'am." He placed his hand on the phone. "May I call and order you anything while you wait?"

"Sue, honey," the woman said to the athletically-built, blond-haired woman who walked up and stood next to her. "Can you wait for a few minutes?" Deb smiled and raised an eyebrow, "Or has withdrawal begun already?"

"You're about as funny as a shark attack." Sue slipped her hand into Deb's hand. "I think I'll survive. But remember," she imitated a serious tone, "if I don't survive, remember to sprinkle my ashes over the Fox News network headquarters." Inseparable since the day they met ten years earlier through a "W4W" posting on match dot com, Debra Gilman and Susan Letterman loved and were dedicated to one another.

They were visiting San Francisco for the first time. The trip was the prize Deb won on the *Wheel of Fortune* game show for solving the prize puzzle. She guessed, "The City by the Bay" with just three T's, two H's, two Y's, and a C showing. "At the end of the show, you saw how Vanna hugged me," Deb would tease. "I think she has a thing for me."

It had been a full year since the game show appearance, yet it took that much time to prepare for the trip. To make the most of their visit to California, they had saved up all of their vacation time, and unless they were physically unable to get themselves to work and remain conscious and upright while there, they avoided taking any sick days. Deb a project manager at a bank and Sue, the activities director at a home for the elderly, made enough money to live nicely, and they were determined to make this a trip of a lifetime. After spending time in San Francisco, they planned to rent a car and drive down the Pacific Coast Highway, stopping in Santa Barbara and Los Angeles, then visit Disneyland before heading home to Chicago.

San Francisco was about more than just sightseeing for the couple. It had taken some effort, but Deb managed to secretly secure an appointment at City Hall, and have their oldest friends Franny and Kela meet them there on Monday afternoon at two o'clock. Deb and Susan's dream to be married in San Francisco was about to come true, yet Susan had no idea.

Until Monday, Deb had to "play it cool" and enjoy their full itinerary. Outfitted with comfortable hiking shoes and daypacks secured, they were ready to trek over and through the parks, hills, and bridges of the city. And each night they planned to visit a different bar or restaurant that they had read about in the *Passport* and *Out* magazines.

Deb pulled a map out of her pocket and handed it to the concierge. "Would you point out on this map how I get to the art galleries around Union Square? And show me how we can get to Chinatown from there." While Phillipe unfolded the complimentary map and drew a line high-lighting the path, Sue sized up the concierge. "He's family," she whispered and nodded to Deb, indicating that she thought the concierge was gay. "Excuse me," Sue asked. "Could you recommend any bars? I mean, that is, if you don't mind sharing." She winked. Phillippe harrumphed. This happened all of the time. *I am French, not gay*, he grumbled to himself.

"Certainly mademoiselle," he answered with a strained smile. He pulled a leaflet from the rack behind him. "Listed under gay nightlife you will find a number of night spots. If you are interested in daytime activity, I would suggest the Castro District. It is what you would call 'cool.'"

"Speaking of cool," Deb interrupted, "I thought this was California. Isn't it supposed to be warm here? I think we need to buy a couple of sweatshirts or something. Is there a gift shop here?"

"Pardon me." A severe-looking woman with a tight ponytail, Superfly sunglasses, and redder-than-red lipstick pushed past Deb and Susan. "I know you won't mind . . . *I'm* in a hurry." She looked them up and down. "Philippe," she turned to the concierge, "where is my car? I ordered a town car." She didn't wait for him to answer. "Why do I bother? If you can't manage to have my car ready then I wonder if I should be staying here."

"Oh, Madame Rothman, I must have made a mistake," he knew he hadn't. "My notes say that you had ordered a car for ten o'clock and it's . . ." he looked at his watch, "it's nine o'clock now. If you would like me to call a car for you right now, I will surely do that."

"Nine, ten, what's the difference? The point is I have an appointment for a manicure and pedicure at ten-ish and I need to pick up a few items at Saks before I go."

"If you will indulge me one minute, Madame Rothman, I will have the valet whistle for a taxi for you." He snapped his fingers at the doorman and pointed to the valet who was standing at the curb.

He turned to Deb and Susan, "Mademoiselles, the *boutique de cadeaux* would be opening in a few moments." He pointed across the lobby at the boutique. "There, at that time, you will be able to purchase a *veste* or a *chandail*. Please let me know if I may assist in any way, and please, for me," he put his hands on his heart, "enjoy your day. Humm?" He smiled. "*Au revoir.*"

"Good morning, everyone." Pamela allowed Maurice, one of the doormen, to take her hand as he guided her up the stairs toward the front doors. "It's a lovely morning, isn't it?" She nodded at Jack who held the door open for her. "Great day, isn't it?" She chirped as she made her way across the lobby toward the front desk staff. "Keys, please. And ooh, who smells so delish? Is that a new fragrance, Candice?"

Attractive and stylish, professional and a genuine people person, Pamela fit into the hotel family perfectly. Pamela loved her job as a sales liaison in the lobby boutique. And why not? It was a happy place, the hotel staff was wonderful, most people were thrilled to be visiting, and it was an easy, straightforward job. Open the doors at nine, help a few customers, go to lunch, and then close the shop at five. The boutique carried what was referred to as upscale leisurewear and fashion necessities. Whether guests needed a wrinkle-free travel skirt, a tankini, silk pajamas, a pair of Spanx, men's socks, or just a simple evening purse, Pamela was there to be of assistance.

Big-ticket items such as designer fashions, watches, jewelry, and cosmetics would bring Pamela an additional two percent commission, but she wasn't there for the money. Three days a week, nine-to-five, she was a part of the lobby family. It was exactly what she wanted and where she wanted to be at this point in her life.

Pamela Spitzer-Ralston the boutique lady didn't need the job—she just wanted to work a few days a week and have the opportunity to meet and interact with new and exciting people who wanted nothing more from her than a smile or advice about what made their butts look too big.

When Pamela turned sixty years old, her life changed. Like Olympic hopefuls or *American Idol* contestants, Pamela had simply "aged out" of the competition. Her turning sixty was the reason—or rather, the excuse—her husband gave for wanting a divorce. Neil, who was sixty-five himself, explained "It's not you, it's me. I need a change. I need 'young.' I need 'active.' I need 'fresh.'" What Neil needed was an excuse to get what Neil wanted: Kimmy, a young, submissive, English-as-(barely)-a-second-language twenty-two-year-old girl with a tight vagina and who was willing the trade it in for a designer purse and a walk-in closet. What he wanted was a self-lubricating groupie who didn't have an opinion.

If anyone ever needed proof that men go through a mid-life crisis, Neil was the poster boy. He bought the yellow Ferrari, a boat, hair implants, capped his teeth, had a perma-tan, wore driving shoes without socks, and had an unlimited refill of Viagra.

The truth was, Neil was a self-serving bore and he did Pamela a favor. She loved him, but she had served her time. After nearly four decades of marriage, she was done. She was bored. When he admitted to having an affair and wanting a divorce, he was surprised by her response. "No hard feelings, Neil. Really," she told him. "The truth is, I'm tired of being married to you too." She explained, "We've been married since I was barely twenty years old. I've had enough. I've been your wife, our children's mother, and have never had a life of my own. I'm running out of time. If I'm ever going to find out what I'm truly made of, I need to be free from the responsibility of tending you, Neil—your needs, your laundry, your moodiness, and heaven knows how many ailments you have."

"Good luck to Kimmy, his twelve-year-old bride," she once told her friends as she lifted her martini in a toast. "All I can say is: enjoy his irritable bowel syndrome, his flakey psoriasis, and good luck ignoring his unending flatulence."

Everyone was happy. Neil was happy with his prepubescent toy. Kimmy, his new young bride who carried designer bags and wore expensive shoes, was happy. And Pamela was free.

Relieved and grateful, Neil was more than generous. He gave Pamela a monthly stipend which paid for a stylish and comfortable apartment and enough money to do whatever she wanted and buy whatever she needed. They were pleasant and amicable when they saw each other at family events, but otherwise they wished each other well and went their separate ways.

At sixty, not only was she paroled from her marriage, but she had also been laid off of her job, fired as a perfume wholesaler. She had thirty-five years of experience and fifteen with the last company, an exemplary sales record, and she made a bonus every year. She had prided herself on a career built on a personal touch and professionalism. But over the years, she witnessed the corporate world turn into a cutthroat, impersonal, and email-driven churn and burn, and the company she worked for decided to restructure itself into a "younger and more vibrant company with cutting-edge and more energetic resources." And with that, Pamela was out of a job.

As part of her dismissal, Pamela was offered a laughable four-week severance package that was contingent upon her spending her last six weeks "transitioning" her clients and training her replacement. "Oh, no thank you," Pamela responded sweetly. She then instructed the Human Resource Director to kiss her ass. "By the way," she added on her way out the door, "the company-issued computer, iPhone, and client files will be placed in the trunk of the company car and it will be parked on the street in front of my house. You'll have three days to arrange for one of your 'energetic resources' to come and retrieve it or I'll consider it abandoned and have it ticketed and towed." She smiled. "Have a nice day."

"Isn't that a little short-sighted, Pamela? Don't you think you owe it to the company?" Trish Mercer, the twenty-eight-year-old MBA-holding, paradigm-hugging Human Resource Director asked. "I'm afraid we won't be able to give a positive recommendation if someone calls for one. Do you want to rethink your decision?"

"Nope, you'll have to figure it out, and I don't think I'll be going on any interviews. I would hardly think that at sixty years old I'll be rebooting my career." What Trish didn't count on was that a woman of a certain age, a woman like Pamela, was not the slightest bit intimidated by a corporate pissant and no longer cared about what people thought of her.

She breathed easier now. The way she was cast aside, riffed, right-sized out of her positions both as sales manager and wife only vindicated her. It was time to make a change and put herself first. She downsized from the big house, filled with service people, expensive cars, impersonal dinner parties, and a high-maintenance husband. She was now unencumbered, unmarried, and living in a cozy apartment walking distance from her favorite shops and restaurants and her longtime friends.

To fill her days, Pamela Spitzer-Ralston took a job at the hotel lobby boutique. It was just a short bus ride from her apartment, an hourly job that paid slightly above minimum wage but it included lunch in the hotel's dining room. Her part-time hours were 9:00 a.m. to 5:00 p.m. three days a week and it was perfect for her.

Each day that she worked in the boutique, Pamela would board the 8:40 a.m. bus on the corner and ride the two stops to the hotel. Depending on the day, she was greeted by either Jack and Maurice or Saul and Dwayne, the doormen who bowed and opened the doors for her as she entered.

On Monday, Wednesday, and Friday mornings Pamela's first duty was to pick up the keys and cash drawer for the boutique at the front desk. Always welcomed with a smile by generally happy people, it was a far cry from having to deal with the self-serving, moody, self-important department store buyers she used to call on.

Without fail, Pamela was greeted by a single flower near the boutique's security gate lock. She had a secret admirer, but gave it little thought. But on this day, there was a note attached to the rose. *Miss Pamela. I would like to invite you to have dinner with me tonight. I will be at the hotel around 6:00 p.m. I hope you are available. Hal, the florist.* She picked up the flower and sniffed the exquisite fragrance as she opened the rolling gates. She flipped on the light switch, placed the cash drawer in the register, and then she sat down and waited. She just waited. That's it . . . she waited. It wouldn't take long before the hotel guests made their way into the shop. They were a captive audience. Whether it was just to browse, waste time, or to look for a specific item, they came to Pamela. They always did.

Pamela read the note again and smiled. When she looked up, she noticed two guests approaching. "Hello, ladies. My name is Pamela. Please let me know if I can I assist you with anything."

"I think I'm going to need a jacket. I thought this was California. I can't believe how cold it is here." Susan looked around the boutique. It was a little ritzy for her taste. "I wasn't planning on buying a new coat. I mean, it *is* August."

Deb took a cotton pullover shirt off the rack and looked at the price tag. "Two hundred and fifty dollars?"

"Yes," Pamela smiled. "San Francisco's weather is always a surprise. Maybe you don't need a coat. What do you have planned while you're here?"

"Well, nothing where we would need to wear a two hundred and fifty dollar T-shirt." Deb turned to Susan, "You were right, Suz. We should have brought heavier clothes."

"Don't worry. I think I can help you." Pamela smiled. "So tell me, what's on your agenda?"

Deb pulled out her list and read it to Pamela.

"Okay. So it's a casual type of day. That sounds nice. Before you buy anything, tell me. What did you ladies bring with you? If I may, I'd like to suggest that you layer."

"Layer?"

"Listen," Pamela leaned in closer, "I could stand here and try to sell you overpriced items, but I'm not interested in doing that. Instead, go back up to your room and layer. Unless you're going to opening night at the symphony or a fancy-schmancy restaurant, smart casual is acceptable anywhere in this city. So, start with a lightweight pullover cotton shirt, top that with a heavier shirt or blouse, then maybe a down vest or a sweater, a scarf, and a fleece or nylon jacket to hold in the heat. That way you can pull on or take off layers as the day warms up and the night cools down and it's all pretty lightweight." She pointed to Deb's backpack. "That will be perfect to hold your clothing. Then you're set."

Deb nodded at her partner, "I think we can do that. I mean, I think we have everything but the scarves." Then she looked over at the shelves filled with silky colorful scarves.

Pamela shook her head and smiled. "If you go up about three blocks and make a left, on the corner you'll find a

Ross Dress for Less. Just pop in there and get the few things you need. Don't spend your vacation dollars at the hotel boutique. It's for pretentious people who have too much money, anyway."

They thanked Pamela. Susan turned to Deb, "Remind me. When we get home we need to work on becoming pretentious."

"Trust me, pretention isn't all that cracked up to what it's supposed to be. As a matter of fact, I think it's pretty obnoxious." Pamela walked them out of the boutique and waved. "Have fun, ladies."

"Oh Miss, Miss! May I get your assistance, please?" Mademoiselle Rothman dramatically swept through the boutique's entrance, wearing her enormous sunglasses and holding her hand in the air as she headed to the cosmetics area. "I must have some of the Chanel Sublimage cream immediately. I left mine at home . . ." She looked around and found that she was standing alone at the counter. "Miss!" she snapped her fingers. "Can we hurry it up, please? I have a mani-pedi in ten minutes."

Pamela smiled and walked over. The woman in the jumbo sunglasses resembled a fly. She was bent over the case, tapping on the glass with her finger. "Finally!" she sounded exasperated. "There," she pointed, "the Chanel Sublimage."

"Yes, ma'am. Will there be anything else?"

The woman straightened up and removed her sunglasses. "Pamela? Pamela, is that you?"

"Yes. Oh, hello, Bunnie." It was Bunnie MacIntosh-Smith-Rothman. She was the fourth wife of an old well-moneyed friend of Neil, Pamela's ex-husband. "How are you? Would you like anything other than the Sublimage?"

Bunnie looked around. "Oh Pamela, this must be mortifying for you. Do you *work* here?"

"Yes, I do . . ." she opened the display case.

"Oh, you poor thing. Neil is a prick, isn't he? This is what has become of you while he is off with that young woman, buying her everything she wants, vacationing, wining and dining her, and you're working as a shop girl. Oh, this is awful. If you tell me that you have started using coupons I may just breakdown right here and cry."

"Don't be so dramatic, Bunnie. This is my choice. I enjoy it." She wanted to change the subject. Besides, Bunnie's concerns were not genuine. Now that she knew where Pamela was, this face cream procurement excursion had turned into a recon mission, to be reported to the ladies at lunch.

"What are you doing here?" Pamela asked. "Are you staying at the hotel?" Her presence seemed odd because she and her husband Ed owned a mega-mansion less than a mile away.

"Renovations!" Bunnie waved her hand in the air. "If Ed thinks I'm going to stay in that house during all of the tumult of re-caulking the tub in the maid's quarters, he is out of his mind." She continued, "He went to New York to meet with his business manager, then he has one of those manly golf weekends or God knows what else, so I came here for a little R and R."

Pamela almost laughed out loud. R and R from what? Lip injections? Kegels? Bunnie was oblivious. The irony of Bunnie was both laughable and cruel. Not only was it during one of those "manly golf weekends" that Neil met his new bride Kimmy, but five years earlier Bunnie met and snatched up Ed while he was on one of those boys-only junkets. At the time, he was married to his third wife. However, that fact didn't keep Bunnie from offering to tee up his balls.

"I must tell you before you hear it from anyone else." Bunnie *tried* to look concerned, but the muscles in her face were frozen in time by Botox. "Yes, it's true." She feigned shame. "Ed and I have been socializing with Neil and Kimmy. But," Bunnie reached for Pamela's hands, "you do know that my allegiance is to you, Pamela dear—it always has been. But what can I do? You know Ed and Neil, they're so tight."

"Oh, yes. They are, aren't they?" Pamela smiled; she didn't actually care. Besides, Kimmy seemed nice enough, Neil seemed happy and, until that moment, Pamela had forgotten all about Bunnie, clearly not having missed that friendship for a moment.

"I'm having lunch with Frieda, Olivia, Prima, and Nona today. You must come. One-ish? At the Mark."

"Oh, no thank you, Bunnie, I'm working." She reached into the display case and pulled out the cream that Bunnie needed.

"Oh well. You'll be missed." She switched subjects. There was more information to gather. "I hear that you moved to a smallish apartment *off* the hill. I just don't think I could do it."

"You'd be surprised, Bunnie. Downsizing is fabulous. I have just what I need. I left the rest with Neil. I don't feel guilty about ridiculous excesses or anything for that matter. I am on my own and loving it." She rang up the sale. "That will be three hundred ninety dollars and ninety-five cents plus tax. Room charge?"

"Of course." Bunnie huffed as if Pamela's was a rhetorical question. "But a shop girl? Weren't you a big sales executive or something?" She shook her head, took the bag from Pamela and said under her breath, "I never could figure out why you did *that* for all of those years, especially when you didn't have to. I could just cry for you."

"Yes, Bunnie. I'm a shop girl." She smiled and walked Bunnie to the entrance of the shop. "Just think. If I didn't work here, you would not have run into me today, and you wouldn't have had anything to tell the girls at lunch."

Pamela walked back into the shop, picked up the note and flower, and she made her decision. She would have dinner with Hal, the florist.

10:00 A.M.

"Good morning, Mr. Pasternak. How are you this morning?" Candice called out to Oscar Pasternak, a long-time resident of the upper floors. "I'll call Marisol and have her deliver your tea and toast to you. Where will you be sitting today?"

Oscar pointed at a sitting area, just to the left of the front desk. "I'll be over here today, watching the world go by. Is the newspaper here yet?"

Oscar Pasternak, a retired actor, had made the Shipley Hotel his home since the early 2000s. When the studios began putting makeup on younger, more popular actors to make them look like senior citizens, his work had dried up and he decided to hang up his comedy and tragedy masks and become an observer, occasionally offering color commentary about what he saw. With the exception of a commercial here and there for a walk-in bathtub, supplemental insurance, or hearing aids, he was no longer in demand. It didn't bother him, though. He was occasionally recognized, and sometimes people would sit down with him to ask questions about his career and leading ladies or just ask to have their picture taken with him. It was enough for him these days.

"I kissed them all," he'd say, "I even slipped the tongue to Susan Sarandon. Man oh man, she was something," and added, "she still is. I should give her a call."

Oscar used the lobby as his living room. He ate his meals there, read the newspaper, socialized, and much to the dismay of the management, he more than occasionally had his afternoon nap there, while the guests and staff went about their business.

Oscar repositioned his favorite lobby chair and settled in for a day of sightseer-seeing.

Bernice, now eighty years old, had a tight gray perm and wore sensible shoes and a cardigan sweater. She sat politely on the lobby sofa with her hands folded around the handbag in her lap. She admired the fabric on the couch and the throw pillows, and then she looked at the lamps and gently tapped on the table. "Real wood," she said to herself. "It must be impossible to keep clean." When she glanced at the front desk Candice smiled and Bernice offered a "How do you do?" Her eyes twinkled when she smiled, just like all grandmas' eyes do.

She noticed someone watching her from across the lobby. "Lloyd," she whispered to her husband, "Isn't that whatshisname?" She gestured at Oscar Pasternak.

"Oh yeah. It's Oscar something-or-another. He's been around forever. I loved his war movies. *That* was when men were men." Lloyd waved at him. "Bernie, do you remember how great he was in that Life Alert commercial?"

Bernice glanced at the time on her tiny black leather banded Timex watch and exhaled. "Maybe we should have called them before we came down from the room."

Lloyd, Bernice's husband of fifty-six years, stood impatiently looking out the window, jingling the change in his pockets. A retired grocer who loved his wife as much as the day they married, he asked, "Bernie, my love, what time did they say they'll come and get us?"

"It should be anytime, dear," she answered sweetly. "Why don't you come and sit by me. Did you take your medication?"

Lloyd knew he shouldn't, but he dreaded the long day ahead. They had traveled across the country to visit their daughter Diane, Jack her husband, and the grandchildren Ashley and Brandon who were spoiled rotten, demanding, and self-centered. Their parents were no better.

Diane, their forty-two-year-old daughter had been a late-in-life child for Lloyd and Bernice. Having thought that they would never have children, Diane was a surprise. They didn't have much money, but they managed, giving her everything they could and providing a stable and loving childhood. They lived in a modest suburban ranch house and sent her to public schools, took family vacations to national parks and places of interest and to Disneyland. Like her friends, Diane had a new Schwinn bicycle every few years, she hosted sleepovers, went to camp, had braces on her teeth, and she got a new wardrobe every year before the school term started. Lloyd and Bernice even took out loans to send Diane to the college of her choice. Still, it seemed impossible to please her. She pouted and whined for eighteen years. By the time Jack, their son-in-law, took Diane off their hands, Bernice and Lloyd were exhausted. That was when they sold their house and moved to a retirement village in Florida, and to insure their sanctuary, they chose a one-bedroom condominium in an adults-only community.

Always claiming to have scheduling or dog-sitting problems, Diane and Jack insisted that Bernice and Lloyd make the hard trip across country "if you want to see your grandchildren." Yet, every visit invitation was peppered with tones of it being an inconvenience; either their house was undergoing reconstruction, or the dog was sick, or they had unbreakable plans. Bernice and Lloyd quickly learned that it would just be easier if they stayed at a hotel, rather than in the cluttered guestroom at Diane and Jack's.

During their last visit, Bernice and Lloyd were treated like unappreciated, addlepated groupies. After a quick lunch out, Bernice and Lloyd spent the day climbing in and out of the back seats of a Range Rover while they were shuttled around to shopping malls, soccer, ballet, taekwondo practices, and computer classes. The day was capped off with being left in Diane and Jack's new, big house to babysit the kids while they went to a party. Lloyd referred to their treatment as human trafficking.

"I hope that Diane and Jack have reined in those kids. The last time we were here they nearly killed us with the running around and jumping." Lloyd said as he looked at his watch again.

"I was afraid for my life." Bernice smiled knowingly at her husband. "How many hissy fits do you think we'll witness this trip?"

Ashley, who was eleven years old, insisted on being the center of attention. She threw tantrums so enormous and violent that she upset herself to point of throwing up. Her parents maintained that she was a sensitive child, but Bernice and Lloyd didn't buy it. Ashley knew how to manipulate her parents. And rather than disciplining her, Diane and Jack just gave in. If Ashley wanted new clothes, an iPad, or a European vacation, they would purchase it for her as quickly as humanly possible, just to avoid an ugly scene which usually occurred in a public place. Hell, if Ashley wanted a pet wolverine, they would have found one on EBay, bought it, and had it express mailed for overnight delivery.

"You don't understand," Diane would justify using a condescending tone. "Parenting is very different these days. We don't punish. We encourage a thoughtful exchange. We listen to our children." Her message was not lost on Lloyd and Bernice. Diane made it clear that she thought her upbringing was stifled and less than optimal. "If I had the freedom that kids do today, who knows what I could have accomplished."

Their grandson, Brandon, excelled at running and jumping on and off of furniture, people, animals, and other things such as ketchup packets while making explosion, screeching tire, or vomit noises. He specialized in sneaking up on people and screaming at the top of his lungs. This left poor Lloyd with what he called PGSD, "Post-Grandchild Stress Disorder." He was jumpy for the four weeks following every visit.

"Oh, and if they ask for money one more time, I'm taking them out of the will," Lloyd grumbled. "Is the bar open?" He looked around. "Maybe we should each have a stiff one before they get here."

Bernice opened her purse and showed Lloyd what was inside. It was a flask. "Don't worry, we're covered." She closed her purse again and let out a thoughtful sigh. "We can't be all that surprised, because our little Diane was a handful when she was young. I think we spoiled her. She was a . . ." She paused.

"She was a monster." They said it at the same time.

"Ungrateful little shit, wasn't she?" Lloyd shook his head.

"Oh yes." Diane agreed. "Then she married that jerk."

Lloyd nodded, "He's an asshole, isn't he? Always has been. What did she see in him, anyway?"

"I'm not sure. I think I remember something about his family having money." Bernice shook her head. "To be honest, who else would put up with Diane? I think she's allergic to work and has the common sense of three year old. We should be grateful he took her off of our hands."

"As long as we're speaking honestly," Lloyd smirked, "I certainly hope that little Ashley has outgrown that homely stage. Based on that kid's forehead and long, gangly arms, I think Jack is part gorilla."

When they arrived twenty minutes late, Diane and the kids rushed into the lobby and Diane administered cursory air-kisses. There weren't any lingering hugs, or tender cheek kisses, no "It's nice to see you," or, "How was your flight?" Just "Come on, mom and dad, get your things. Jack is double parked."

Brandon ran through the lobby then over to the front desk where he emptied the complimentary apple bowl onto the floor and made the sound of a machine gun firing. He then skipped over to the lobby couches where he proceeded to jump on one then the other. When he was finished there, he ran across the lobby to the brochure rack where he promptly pulled out handfuls of maps and pamphlets and threw them on the floor.

"Grandma, grandma, grandma, grandma . . . *grandma!*" Ashley became more insistent.

"What!" Bernice snapped. "I mean, what is it, dear?"

"Did you know that I am in advanced classes because I'm *exceptional*. In fact, *I* go to a private school. I have a blog where I write down my thoughts and I have two hundred and fifty-two Facebook friends. Do you have a Facebook page? I'll friend you, and you can see all the great stuff I do."

"Okay, dear." Bernice was already overwhelmed even though it had only been a few minutes since the kids had arrived.

Looking down at her phone, Ashley held up her hand and then shushed Bernice. "I can't talk to you right now. I need to text my friends."

"I see that Brandon still has a lot of energy," Lloyd said pointing at Brandon who was now at the concierge's desk, trying to pull the phone away from him. The concierge was looking at Diane with pleading eyes.

"Brandon, honey," Diane called out in a whisper. "Let's you and I meet in the middle of the lobby, where we can compromise. It's a safe midway point where we can discuss three reasons why you think the concierge won't let you use his phone."

"Because he's a cocksucker," Brandon yelled back.

"Now, Brandon, isn't that a word that's on our do-not-use list?"

"It's two words, moron!" Then he held up his hands and he flipped his mother off. "Ker-pow!"

"Hey, young man!" Lloyd reprimanded him. "That's no way to speak to your mother . . ."

Diane put her hand on Lloyd's arm. "We do not reprimand our children. We think it is counterproductive. We think that it's important that they express themselves freely. It builds confidence. We like to let them monitor themselves."

"That's a load of crap. Have you *tried* parenting? It was a popular concept for decades." He then turned to his wife and said under his breath, "I'm not sure I'm up for this today."

"Mom, Dad? Did you bring him a gift?" Diane nodded her head. "I'm sure he would be interested in that."

"We don't know what children like nowadays." Bernice explained. "We brought them savings bonds. They can put them in the bank and use them for college."

"That's okay." Hardly listening, Diane looked at her watch. "We can stop at the toy store and let them pick out what they want."

Brandon had moved across the lobby and was now entertaining himself by flicking the backside of Oscar Pasternak's newspaper as he was reading it.

After a minute passed, Oscar folded down his newspaper, leaned forward, and whispered, "Listen, little boy, if you don't knock that off right now, I'm going to tear your arm off at the elbow and beat you with it. Now fuck off, you little bastard."

It actually startled Brandon, but still he managed to yell, "You're a whore, man," as he walked away.

Lloyd asked, "What do we have planned for today, Diane? Do I need to get my running shoes?"

"No, but we need to hurry because the kids have a swim party today and we need to drop them off in less than an hour. I have a million things to do, the dog is already at the groomers, and Jack needs to get to his office. We'll just pick something up for dinner because Jack will most likely be working late. Think about it. Do you want Mexican, chicken, hamburgers? It's up to you." She chirped, "You can let me know but," she paused, "remember Ashley thinks she's a vegan now."

Bernice looked confused. "Diane, may I ask you a question?"

"What is it, mom? We're in a hurry." She said it over her shoulder as she tried to wave the kids over.

"Diane," Bernice's face turned red and she sat down. "Why did you invite us to come? We made this trip to spend time with you and the family. These arrangements were made months ago, and now you're telling me that the kids have other plans to go to a party, Jack seems to be avoiding us, and we're being hustled around like our visit is an inconvenience."

Diane seemed surprised that her mother, who had always been so calm and accommodating, not only appeared to be upset, but she spoke up about it. "Mom, I'm sorry." She took a deep breath. "I don't think you understand . . ."

Just then Jack stomped into the lobby. "What is taking so long? Now I have to pay the valet." He looked at Bernice and Lloyd. "Hey Lloyd, do you have any cash?" He didn't wait for an answer. He looked at Diane again. "I told you . . ."

"Jack, take the kids to the car and I'll be there in a minute."
She stopped herself, "Better yet, why don't you take the kids
to the party and go to work from there. I'll take a cab."

"Come on, you little shits," Jack barked. "Get in the car."

Suddenly, Diane looked sad and defeated. She sat down
next to her mother and patted the couch, indicating that she
wanted her father to sit down too.

"Mom, Dad. I know it seems like we're not making any
time for you, but we have so much going on." She looked as
if she was about to cry. "*I* really wanted to see you. I did. And
I need your advice."

Diane began explaining. "As you can see, the kids are a
handful. You'll thank me, trust me. Because after you spend
about five minutes with them you'll *want* them to be somewhere else. And I know," she continued, "that Jack appears to
be pretty self-involved. It's just that things are tough for us
right now."

Lloyd looked at Bernice with a knowing look. He was
certain that Diane was going to ask to borrow money again.
"Here we go." He stood up.

"No. It's not what you think. It's just that," tears began
rolling down her cheeks, "everything is out of control. Jack
insists that it's just a phase. Even if it is, I don't know what
to do. I'm lost." She sniffed and wiped her eyes. "We hardly
have any savings. And you know I gave up my career to raise
the children."

"You had a career?" Lloyd never remembered Diane
having a job of any kind, let alone a career.

Bernice shushed her husband and turned to her daughter. "When did all of this happen? You always told us things
were good."

"Great, in fact," Lloyd added. "I never really believed it,
but I took your word for it." He remembered the last visit
when Jack took him into the garage to show him his "toys."

There were new bicycles, scooters, sports gear, surf boards, kitchen appliances, and although he never played golf, Jack had a new set of golf clubs. He justified the purchase by explaining that he thought that he might like to try it someday. And even though Jack bragged that they have the best gardening crew in town to maintain their landscaping, he had a new riding tractor mower. To top it off, Jack had hired a professional garage organizer to build shelves and cabinets to house all of his "toys" *and* return four times a year to "maintain placement."

"It's taken me a long time to face the truth. I think we just allowed everything to happen." She sniffed, "I thought I was doing the right things, but now I realize that I have made some serious mistakes and I need to know how to fix things."

"Oh, thank God." Bernice smiled at Lloyd and sat back relieved. "We thought you had become the most obnoxious, most ungrateful woman on earth, and trust me," she patted her daughter's knee and nodded toward Lloyd, "your father has been looking into changing our phone number. But don't worry, honey. Things can't be all that bad."

"Sure they can." Lloyd interrupted. "But almost everything can be fixed one way or another, or not. In any case, we'll help if we can." Lloyd flagged down a staff member and whispered, "I have an extra twenty dollar bill for you if you could you do me a favor and bring me a Bloody Mary with an extra shot."

For the next half an hour, Diane sat with her parents and explained that Jack was on the verge of losing his job again, and that he not only worked late most evenings, he also needed to report to the office during the weekends. "Jack's not avoiding you. He's in trouble and he's embarrassed." She explained that they were in debt. The kid's private schools tuitions were more than they could afford and after catering to them for so many years, the children had turned into uncontrollable, sucking black holes of entitlement.

"They're even worse than I was," she conceded with a weak smile. "For the first several years of our marriage and after Jack's father passed away, we had a lot of money. We spoiled ourselves, spending like drunken sailors and congress. I have to admit, I got used to it. I liked living like a princess. I loved it. But we may have gone overboard. After the kids were born I never went back to work and," she admitted, "Jack has never been very ambitious. He loses or leaves one job after another and now the money has run out. Jack and I argue constantly. I feel useless and I simply don't know what to do." She continued, "I know you and Dad didn't have a lot of money. But you always figured out how to manage and seemed happy while you did it."

"Are you asking for our advice?" Lloyd was leery.

"I guess I am. But," she warned them with a smile, "be gentle because we all know how *I* can be."

"First, you have to stop feeling sorry for yourself, dear. We all get in a bind from time to time. Just break it down and deal with one thing at a time."

"You need to sit down with Jack and work out a plan and a budget." Lloyd looked at Bernice, "What do they call it these days? Unclutter, declutter? Resize? Oh, who knows anymore. There's always a new way of saying things. Remember the words 'hobo' and 'crippled' and 'retarded'? Who can keep up? In any case, in my day we simply called it 'cutting back,' or 'living within your means.'" Lloyd tried to refocus. "Sell the house and move to a smaller one—or an apartment, if you need to."

Bernice took over. "You, Diane, I think you need to get out there and get a job. It will help to rebuild your confidence."

"And tell that husband of yours to be man-ish." Lloyd barked.

"That's 'man up,' Lloyd." Bernice turned back toward her daughter and continued. "What your father is saying is that your husband should grow a pair and 'man up,' dear. And take the kids out of private school, and . . ."

Lloyd chimed in again. "Stop all the high-priced lessons. Odds are that Ashley and Brandon are not going to grow up and be ballerinas or concert violinists or soccer players. I'm not an anthropologist, but I don't think that studying and helping around the house has killed anyone."

"Yes, Diane dear, I hate to point out the obvious, but you can see that none of their extracurricular activities are really helping with their social skills. Those kids need to know that you can't afford everything. Teach them some realistic values. Let them go to public school and be around kids who are not overly privileged for a while. You'll see—they'll become better behaved and more appreciative."

"Or," Lloyd added, "get the snot beaten out of them. It only needs to happen once."

"I know," Diane shrugged. "It all makes sense, but the kids are used to..."

"The word 'no' works wonders. If they don't like it, then that's too bad," Lloyd suggested. "And if they don't listen, then . . . what do they call it now? Put 'em down?"

"No, dear," Bernice corrected him. "It's called 'put them in a time out,' not 'put them down.' That's what you do to rabid dogs." Lloyd shrugged.

"I'm afraid if I put them in a time out every time they misbehaved, they would be in the corner until they're in their late twenties."

"That sounds like a good plan," Lloyd clapped his hands together. "Put 'em down."

11:00 A.M.

Other than a yearly weekend trip to the rodeo in northern Arizona and a few overnighters when an event was just too far from home for it to be a day trip, their honeymoon was the only planned vacation Clark and Nancy March had ever taken.

Where did the time go? It seemed like just yesterday when high school sweethearts Clark March and Nancy Helgeson got married. But it had been thirty years. They were just kids in 1986, living in McNary, Arizona, when two days after their high school graduation they drove one hundred and ninety-eight miles up to Phoenix to be married at the courthouse. After the ten-minute ceremony, witnessed by their best friends, Wallace Hunts and Dolly Dettmeyer, they all celebrated with lunch at TGI Fridays. It seemed so decadent. They ordered appetizers: deep fried zucchini. Clark ordered a steak and Nancy had an order of loaded potato skins and they shared, giddy knowing that this is how married people did it.

When they walked to the parking lot and said their good-byes, Nancy ceremoniously tossed her handmade wedding bouquet of silk and plastic flowers to Dolly who told her "You're the luckiest girl in the world" as they hugged farewell.

Clark and Nancy drove through the night to Las Vegas for their honeymoon. They checked in to the La Conquistador Motor Inn, which was off the strip, and parked their rusty old pickup truck just outside the door of their room. It was a worn-down, crappy room with off-kilter tattered drapes that hung precariously, barely covering the grimy window. The bed was small and lumpy and the musty smell coming from the bathroom was still more appealing than the green, slimy swimming pool. But to the newlywed couple it was paradise. After two days, they returned to Arizona and moved into an inexpensive studio apartment in Mesa. They were ready to begin their lives together as the Marches.

For thirty years, money was tight for Clark and Nancy March. Frivolous spending was never a consideration. They worked very hard, rarely complained, and managed to build a beautiful family: Joe, who was now twenty-nine, Meg (twenty-eight), Amy (twenty-six), and Beth (twenty-four). Their four children were their focus, and any money beyond rent, necessities, and medical bills was put into the college account. Although neither Clark nor Nancy attended college, they were determined to help their children identify and achieve their goals. Clark and Nancy were so proud. They truly felt that their children's happiness and success was theirs too. They instilled love, loyalty, and ambition in their four children. "I can't help them with long division and my spelling is pretty bad," Clark used to say. "But I can teach them to be good people." And he did.

Clark and Nancy were about to celebrate their thirtieth wedding anniversary, so Joe and his sisters pooled their money and presented their parents with this trip to San Francisco as a surprise gift. As far as they were concerned, their parents deserved much more.

Watching them interact, it was clear that the Marches were not only dedicated to one another after all of these years, but they were still in love. They were so authentically sweet, gentle, and thoughtful of each other that it made strangers stop and take notice.

For as long as they could remember, Clark and Nancy had wanted to visit San Francisco. Sometimes at night, while they lay in bed before drifting off to sleep, they'd talk about their imagined visit. Nancy would describe a romantic walk along the bay at sunset. "And the boat ride," Clark would add, "the one that goes under the Golden Gate Bridge. We would need to take a jacket. I hear it gets windy."

"Do you know what I want?" Nancy blushed in the darkness, "I want a huge ice cream cone at Ghirardelli Square."

Until this trip, it was only make believe and that was okay for them. They had a simple life with bills to pay. "Sometimes a dream is better." Nancy would say, "It never has to end."

When the travel plans were set Clark contacted his oldest daughter Meg. "I want to do something special for your mom on our anniversary. She deserves it. Raising you kids and putting up with me for all of these years . . ." He cleared his throat, "Meg honey, could you go with me to Zales jewelry store at the mall? I want to buy your mom the engagement ring that I never gave her. She says it don't matter . . ." He continued, "Anyways, I could use your help."

Clark asked his boss at Benson's Car Repair for the afternoon off of work. "If she calls," he instructed his coworkers, "be sure you tell Nancy that I had to go deliver a car." He hated having to lie but it was for a good cause.

Meg drove her dad to the mall as they had planned. What surprised her was the wad of ten, twenty and hundred dollar bills Clark pulled out of his pocket. When he saw the shocked look on her face he knew he needed to explain. "Oh, I didn't steal it or nothing." He blushed. "I've been saving part or all of my lunch money for over two years. And sometimes Mr.

Benson has a little side work for me. I've been planning to do something like this for a long time."

"Dad," Meg laughed. "We shouldn't be a Zales. We should be a Tiffany's." The reference was lost of Clark.

The jeweler approached, "Hello sir, I'm Dennis. What can I do for you today?"

"Oh hello, sir. I would like to buy an engagement ring." Clark reached into his pocket and pulled out a crumpled piece of notebook paper. "I looked at your web site and I think I know what I would like." He straightened the paper. "I would like to see the three-quarter carat total weight, certified diamond three-stone ring in fourteen karat white gold." He looked up. "Size six, please."

"Well, sir, you certainly seem prepared. Is the ring for this lovely lady?" Dennis nodded toward Meg.

"Oh no." He corrected Dennis, "This is Meg—she's my daughter. The ring is for my wife Nancy."

"An engagement ring for your wife? It seems like you have already sealed the deal." Looking Clark up-and-down, Dennis sized him up as a simple blue collar man who could easily be manipulated. "Don't you mean a keepsake ring or something from our Unforgettable Collection?"

"No, sir," Clark insisted. "I know what I want. And I'm sure that my Nancy would love this engagement ring." He pointed to his notes.

Thirty minutes later when they exited the store, Meg asked, "So, dad, have you thought about how you are going to present the ring to mom?"

Clark smiled. As corny as it seemed, Clark loved romance. He and Nancy would dance in the living room, take walks in the rain and hold hands at the movies. "I've thought about this," he said. "I was planning on finding the perfect moment, maybe on a walk in the park or on a cable car or something. I wanna do it on the first day, so we can have kinda have a second honeymoon. But, I'll know when it feels right, and that's when I'll propose to her again. No matter what, it has to be special and memorable."

Although the flight was scheduled to leave Sky Harbor Airport at 8:00 a.m., they were there at the gate at 5:00 a.m. This meant they were up, dressed, packed, and on the road to the airport at three o'clock. Although they were both forty-eight years old, this was the first time either of them had ever been on an airplane. After hearing about all of the TSA security policies and delays at airports, they decided not to take any chances.

Meg had been elected by her siblings to make the special arrangements for their parent's trip, the first being the hotel's town car. The driver would pick them up at the airport when they arrived and bring them to the hotel. She also briefed the hotel concierge about the occasion, explaining that her father was planning on proposing again and she arranged to have champagne served for the occasion. "I'd like to explain why this is so special. You see our parents have been together for thirty years, since they were eighteen years old. They worked incredibly hard to make sure that we had everything we needed. They even managed to put all four of us through college. My brother and sisters and I want to be certain that this is the best trip possible. What can you do to help us achieve that?"

Nancy and Clark held hands and sat quietly throughout the plane ride, staring out the small oval window for the full two-hour trip. When they walked from the plane to the luggage area, they saw a sign with their names on it: "Mr. & Mrs. Clark March." Clark's immediate thought was that they were in trouble for something, although he couldn't think of what it could be. He stepped toward the man holding the sign. He was wearing a black suit and aviator sunglasses and looked very official. Clark cleared his throat and asked timidly, "Excuse me, sir, I'm Clark March. Is there somethin' wrong?"

"No, sir, I'm Fredrick, your driver." He removed his sunglasses and smiled. "The hotel has sent its town car to the airport to collect you. I understand that this is your anniversary and the Shipley Hotel wanted to help kick off your weekend, sir. So, if you'll just hand me your luggage claim tickets, I will collect your bags for you and then we will be off."

While in the car, the driver referenced points of interest during the ride and made small talk. "Please help yourself to water if you are thirsty."

"How much does it cost?"

"Nothing sir, it's complimentary." Fredrick smiled to himself. Clark and Nancy were very refreshing. Their naiveté was something he didn't see very often. More often than not, he had to endure overbearing, entitled, *nouveau riche* jackasses who treated him like he was a rented mule. When he stopped at a traffic light he quickly glanced down at his clipboard. *Oh crap!* He was scheduled to pick up someone with an insipid nickname, clearly some D-, E-, F-, or Q-list celebrity, along with his entourage of morons who will probably be drunk or high. Fredrick pushed the clipboard onto the floorboards and decided to enjoy his current passengers instead of dwell on the headache that would be in his back seat an hour or two later.

"Mr. March, sir." He looked at Clark using the rearview mirror. "Is this your first visit to our city?"

Clark looked at Nancy, they both smiled, embarrassed. "Mr. Fredrick, would you believe this is our first trip anywhere? It's actually the first time either of us have been on an airplane."

"Is that so, sir? Ma'am," he shifted his eyes to Nancy, "How did you enjoy the flight?"

"I don't have anything to compare it to, but I was surprised that everyone sits so closely together. But other than that, everything was very nice."

Nancy sat in the back seat, her hands folded politely and resting on her purse, which was in her lap. Clark was watching her, smiling at how beautiful she was. If she had changed at all during the past thirty years, it was that she became more beautiful in Clark's eyes.

Nancy could feel Clark staring at her as she took in the sights through the window. She smiled to herself. She didn't turn her head but she allowed her hand fall on to the seat. Clark gently reached down and intertwined his fingers with hers. They never let go for the rest of the ride.

"Well, sir. Here we are at the Shipley Hotel. Welcome." Fredrick stopped the car in front of the hotel and informed Clark, "I'll get the door sir." He jumped out of the driver's seat and made his way around the back passenger side and opened the door for the couple. Although unnecessary, Fredrick bowed giving the Marches the full effect. Fredrick snapped his fingers and a bellman rushed over to take the luggage from the trunk.

"Hey, where is he taking that!" Clark was alarmed.

Fredrick caught on. "No worries, sir, that's the bellman, and it's his job to take your bags inside for you."

When Clark reached into his pocket, Fredrick held up his hand. "That is not necessary, sir. It has already been taken care of, and it was my pleasure driving you today." He handed Clark a card. "Please call me if you are in need of a car during your stay."

Clark and Nancy stepped into the lobby. It took their breath away.

"Hello, Miss," Clark said when he stepped up to the desk, "I am Clark March, and I would . . . ."

Barbara looked at her computer screen and smiled. "Oh yes, Mister March. Fredrick called ahead. We have been expecting you. Welcome." She stepped out from behind the desk. "We will be happy to store your luggage until your room is ready. In the meantime, if you wish to use the spa to freshen up, please be our guests." She handed Nancy two passes to the day spa.

"Oh, well . . . a spa?" He whispered to Nancy, "I didn't bring my swim trunks. Maybe we should just head out and start sightseein'."

"Clark, honey, if it's okay with you, I'd like to freshen up and comb my hair and then . . . can we go get some ice cream?" She smiled mischievously and rubbed her hands together as she said it.

Clark watched Nancy as she crossed the lobby and marveled at the grandeur of the room.

"Mr. March, we received a call from your daughter Megan, informing us of the occasion. I would like you to meet our concierge." Barbara led him over to a decorative desk on the outskirts of the lobby. She continued, "This is Philippe. He has made some arrangements for to celebrate your proposal this evening and the hotel would like to provide a bottle of champagne to toast the occasion. So, when you are ready . . ."

Clark shushed them, "Shush, here she comes."

Nancy had put on a fresh T-shirt and pulled on her faded blue STP windbreaker to match the one Clark was wearing.

"You look pretty." He smiled. "Are you ready to go?"

"I sure am." She pointed downward. "See, I have my walking shoes on."

Clark took Nancy's hand and before they walked out he turned to concierge, "Don't worry, we're just going out for a little while. We'll be back." He blushed.

12:00 P.M.

Marisol walked through the lobby carrying a tray. On it there was a plate with a turkey sandwich on rye, and a kosher pickle and a tall glass of iced tea. She set it down on the table near Oscar as he repositioned his chair. Noontime was his favorite part of the day. "It's like a Broadway show," he'd say.

It was just twelve noon: checkout time. The clerks readied themselves for the departing visitors and their stories about lost keys, credit card charge denials, and disputes about minibar and movie charges and the general minute complaints from cranky travelers. During the monthly staff meetings, the management repeated the hotel service mantra. "Continue smiling and do everything in your power to keep the guest happy, assuring a good review and another visit."

Barbara stepped up to her assigned computer at the counter, straightened her skirt, re-tucked her blouse, and buttoned her jacket. In addition to her regular duties, she had been assigned the task of training a newly-hired employee, Francesca. Barbara had been an employee at the hotel for nine years, working her way up from night shift to day desk manager. She took her job seriously—she had to. After graduating with a degree in hotel and restaurant management, not only did she have a mound of college loans, she had a goal: to become the general manager of a prestigious hotel in ten year's time. She had a problem, though. She hated check-out time. She found the guests stories and chatter tedious.

Barbara nodded toward Francesca, eyeing her jacket, and Francesca quickly buttoned hers as well. Earlier she had instructed Francesca that her job was to look every guest in the eye and assure them that it is the hotel's immense plea-sure to host them during their visit and no request was out of reach. Barbara reviewed the process for quickly calling up the guest's information on the computer then reciting it, as if it was memorized and the most important information one could possess. "It makes the guest feel special."

She knew, however, that the hotel chain was offering a special "three nights for the cost of two" deal, and the member points were doubled—which meant that these were bargain hunters and, without a deeply discounted rate, they would probably not be visiting again in the future. "Just beware," Barbara rolled her eyes. "The bargain travelers are the worst. They usually want something for nothing."

The clerks referred to checkout time as rush hour: A traffic jam of rolling luggage and exasperated travelers lined up to check out. Barbara glanced at the people who were queueing up and whispered to her trainee, "Here is a helpful hint. You can always tell when a guest steps up to the counter and already has his reading glasses perched on the tip of his nose and the preliminary bill in his hand that there is going to be a charge dispute."

The first departing guest of the day stepped up to the desk, and Barbara smiled wide. "Hello, ma'am. Did you enjoy your stay with us?"

"Yes, thank you. It was fine." A bloated businesswoman placed her overstuffed purse on the counter, freeing up her hands to adjust her tight-fitting jacket. "I am Donna Osterhauser, and I am ready to check out, please. I have to catch a flight and I'm in a hurry." Donna was a new business traveler. The economy forced her to take a job where she would be on the road seventy-five percent of the time, away from her family and the comfort of her home. This was the first of many business trips to come. In a short few months she would become pasty and haggard from too many hours in the dry air of one plane after another. And she'd be overly tired, with bags under her eyes, practically *living* in hotels. She'll learn that sightseeing and enjoying the city or its restaurants will never be an option, and no matter how big or luxurious the room is or what "superior mattress" a hotel advertises, it will never really be comfortable. But for now, Donna was going to learn her first lesson about being a business traveler.

Barbara perched her fingers over the keyboard. "Room number, please . . . and where are you off to today? Back home? Miss Osterhauser?

"Twelve-oh-four, and yes, I'm headed home, back to Saint Paul." Donna adjusted her blouse. It was gaping between her breasts. She had somehow gained weight during the four-day business trip, but couldn't figure out how. Donna had brought her exercise clothes and used the hotel's treadmill in the mornings, yet by the end of the week all of her clothes were snug and uncomfortable.

"Let me print out your bill for you to review. One minute please." Barbara pressed a button and a minute later she lifted a small stack of pages off of the printer and placed it on the counter. "Here you go, Miss Osterhauser. Would you like to take a look and make sure everything is okay?"

Donna began reviewing the charges. "What's this? *Tomar con...*" She pointed to a line with a $19.99 charge.

"Let me see." Barbara looked at the bill. Oh, that's a movie charge ma'am." She ran her finger across the paper. "It was purchased on the twenty-sixth at 9:12 p.m.."

"A movie?" Donna Osterhauser turned pale. "What movie?"

Barbara pressed a few keys on her computer. "Here it is." She leaned in and whispered, "The movie is called, "*Tomar con Profundo*. Oh . . ." Barbara looked at the screen again and clarified, "That's the Spanish subtitled version. The title in English is *Takin' it Deep*."

"Well," Donna swallowed hard. Her forehead looked damp. She hadn't realized that the actual title of the porno movie would show up on the bill. She couldn't possibly submit it to her company for reimbursement. "I . . . I didn't watch that! This must be a mistake. I don't speak Spanish. I don't even think I was here. As a matter of fact, I think I was out to dinner that night."

The lady doth protest too much, Barbara smiled. "Yes, ma'am. It must be a mistake. We will take it off of your bill." Barbara looked at her computer screen, then pointed at the print out again. "Oh look at that, do we have another error? Do I need to remove charge for *Cock-work Orange*, as well?" Barbara suppressed her laughter, but Francesca's eyes were tearing and she had to excuse herself.

"Yes, and," Donna pointed at an $88.15 charge, "what is this charge?" She pressed her luck.

"That's a room service charge. The order was placed at 8:05 p.m. on the twenty-sixth. It looks like you were here for dinner on the twenty-sixth after all. Oh my, Miss Osterhauser," Barbara looked confused. "Have we made another mistake?"

"Oh, yeah," The color of her face turned crimson. "I guess that one is right."

"And these charges," she pointed to several lines. "What are they?"

"Oh yes, Miss Osterhauser. Those are the minibar restock-ing charges. Let's see," Barbara craned her neck so she could read what Miss Osterhauser was pointing at, then pulled up the charges on her computer screen. "Here we go. There were four vodkas, two Kahluas, a Coke, and a Kit Kat, a Snickers, peanut M&Ms, and a can of Pringles used on the twenty-sixth. And three vodkas, a Baileys Irish Cream, a Diet Coke, plain M&Ms, Jellybellies, Jordan almonds, and a can of Pringles on the twenty-seventh." She took a breath and continued. "And on the twenty-eighth, two Jamesons, two vodkas, a Baileys Irish Cream, one Frangelico, a package of Gummy Bears, mixed nuts, and a can of Pringles. And," she tapped the last charge on the bill, "it looks like a bottle of wine and a giant-size Toblerone was removed from the sensor fridge at 11:50 a.m. today." Barbara looked at the clock hanging on the wall. It read 12:08 p.m.

There was no possible scenario that would allow Donna to submit this bill to her company with an extra five-hundred dollars for porn, liquor, and snacks. "Well, maybe I had a Diet Cola or something, but not any of that other stuff." She became artificially indignant. "What's going on here?" She looked around. "Who is the manager?"

"Oh, ma'am, clearly this must be a mistake. May I offer an apology on behalf of the management?" Barbara employed her practiced sincere facial expression. This was not a new or isolated occurrence of a business traveler racking up charges that she couldn't report. "What I can do is separate out the minibar charges onto another bill and you can use a different credit card if you wish, or you can address those charges with the general manager if that's more convenient." She looked over her shoulder to Francesca. "Francesca, would you please call maintenance and have them send someone up to room twelve-oh-four. There is something wrong with the sensor fridge." She turned back to Donna, "Oh, Miss Osterhauser, thank you for identifying the problem."

"I should say so. Maybe you should check your computer system, or manage your maid service a little more closely . . ." Donna stopped herself. She knew she was ahead of the game . . . this time.

"I will definitely pass along those suggestions." Barbara placed a folded pamphlet on the counter. "It would certainly help us if you would take a minute and complete this customer satisfaction form. And please itemize the errors we made on your bill. That way the management can review each charge and figure out what the heck happened. Then, if necessary, the appropriate staff will be counseled."

"Oh, no, I don't want to get anyone in trouble." The last thing Donna wanted was to have anyone confirm that she did, in fact, watch two porno movies while consuming nineteen thousand calories from the minibar and swiping a bottle of wine as she left the room to check out. "Really, I'd rather not. I don't have any time." She tapped her watchless wrist. "I have to go."

"Are you sure?" Barbara loved this part. She lifted the receiver to the desk phone, "because it's no problem. I can page the general manager to come and speak with you right now. It won't take but a minute."

"Yes, I am sure." Donna nearly tripped over her roller bag as she backed away from the desk. Barbara and Francesca thoroughly enjoyed watching Donna as she rushed to get the hell out of there.

"Okay then, thank you for staying with us. We will look forward to seeing you again." Barbara smiled to herself and placed the customer service satisfaction form down on the desk, then looked up. "May I help the next guest, please?"

Resident Oscar Pasternak stood up and applauded, "Brava, Barbara! That was most enjoyable. I'm not sure Meryl Streep could have done it any better." He looked around and rubbed is hands together. "Who's next?"

1:00 P.M.

They were too nervous to sit down. Instead, Sarah Weinberg and Tony Lucci stood silently, holding each other's hand, eyes focused on the lobby's giant revolving door they waited for both sets of parents to arrive. Now that Tony and Sarah were engaged to be married, it was time for the Weinbergs and Luccis to meet each other. Both twenty five years old and eager to please, they were terrified that their parents wouldn't get along. Tony had planned this brunch, making reservations in the hotel's dining room hoping that meeting in a public place might keep the drama to a minimum.

Sarah's parents were devout-reformed "delicatessen" Jews, or Jews who rarely attended the synagogue yet conveniently became *very* Jewish, speaking Yiddish with an "old country" affect when they were excited and during the holidays. They were the Diet Coke of Judaism, more guilt without all the extra calories.

Tony's folks were overly-affected, situational-convenience Italians who were actually third generation American, but acted like they moved here from Sicily the day before yesterday. They donned thick accents and theatrical hand gestures when food and family were involved.

Unfortunately for the already nervous young couple, both sets of parents were late. The maître d'hôtel was understanding when Tony nervously tried to explain his predicament. "This is such an important lunch for Sarah and I. Hopefully nothing will go wrong." He looked at his watch, "Well, they're already late. This is going to be a disaster."

"Don't worry, Mr. Lucci," Bruno Monsarelli, the maître d'hôtel, calmly assured him. "Why don't you and your lovely fiancé wait in the lobby? I will keep your reservation open and seat your entire party when everyone has arrived." Bruno couldn't help but smile. The young couple reminded him of himself and his bride Gloria, many years earlier when they were so young and in love. "I'll tell you what, Mr. Lucci. The hotel would like to send you a bottle of Prosecco for a toast with the parents. I will have it delivered to the lobby for you."

Tony walked toward Sarah and made a thumbs-up motion. He wanted it to appear that he had taken charge and the whole situation under control.

"What if they don't like each other?" Sarah was worried.

"I hope they do. But it doesn't really matter. Because I love you and that's all that counts." Tony squeezed her hand.

It had been almost two years since Sarah Weinberg and Tony Lucci noticed each other in the elevator of the office building where they worked. Weeks of stolen glances between floors eventually turned into not-so-coincidental meetings in the building's first floor café, and finally culminated into small talk as they waited in line to pay for their coffees. It took an additional six weeks, and gallons of coffee before Tony could work up the nerve to invite Sarah out on a date.

Sarah was relieved and thrilled, but more importantly embarrassment was averted. For weeks, she had been telling her friends and coworkers about "this cute guy" who she had met, yet she couldn't report an invitation to dinner or a movie. She had checked his ring finger—nope, no ring there.

He didn't *seem* gay. But then again, how does one seem gay? In San Francisco, a woman should probably always assume the man is gay until proven otherwise. There was a joke floating around the office. If a single heterosexual woman who lives in San Francisco wants to find a man and get married, there's only one thing she needs to do. She needs to move out of the city of San Francisco.

Her friends offered counsel. "You have to hint," Tiffany Goldbaum told her.

"Hint hard," Christa Monroe chimed in with a wink.

"Better yet," Karen Gardner added, "tell him you don't have plans for the weekend and ask him what he would suggest."

"Or," Lucia Menendez, the most mature and most experienced of the ladies suggested, "Why don't *you* ask *him* out? Men don't understand subtle, they don't understand hinting." She elaborated. "One day early in our marriage, my first husband was watching some hundred-hour sporting event on TV and I wanted some attention. So I stripped down and stood naked in front of the television set. I even did a little provocative dance. Do you know what he said about it? He said, 'Hey, Lucy, while you're up could you make me a sandwich'? So," she concluded, "be bold. Tell him what you want. Say, 'hey handsome, let's have dinner on Friday, I'll meet you at such-and-such restaurant at eight o'clock.'" She clapped her hands together. "No fuss, no muss."

After listening to and weighing everyone's advice, Sarah decided that she would start asking sly probing questions about Tony's weekends and family. She would even offer that she didn't have plans for a particular weekend or evening. It was a ridiculous game, but it seemed to be the only way to engage him in a conversation that lasted longer than the coffee line. Still, weeks went by before Tony caught on.

"I thought you must have had a boyfriend," he admitted during their first date. "I was afraid to ask you out. I didn't want to embarrass myself."

"Well, you should have asked me, silly. I've been dropping hints since our first cup of coffee together. And I don't even like coffee." She laughed, "Oh my goodness, I was light-headed and nauseous for weeks."

It was a sweet courtship. Both shy and inexperienced, they took it slow. It started with casual dates on Saturday nights and occasionally on a Sunday afternoon. They shared polite conversations, walks in the park, and dinners in busy restaurants. Their sweet and polite kisses developed into deep, desire-filled necking on the front porch. But still, despite everyone and everything around them prompting them to do so, after six months and over twenty dates later they still hadn't consummated their relationship.

Sarah began to wonder if she was wasting her time. Despite how much she liked and desired Tony, he just didn't seem able to make his move. She couldn't figure it out. Was it because he lived with his parents? Didn't he know what to do? Was he really gay? Or was it because he simply didn't find her attractive? She decided that there was one way to find out.

"Tony, can I ask you a question?" Sarah asked one night as he was walking her to her front door. "Why haven't you tried to sleep with me? Is there something wrong?"

"Oh no, Sarah." He stopped dead in his tracks. "I want to. I really, really, *really* do. It's just that I didn't want to push you."

"Well," she stepped closer and brushed her lips against his, "*push* me, Tony. Push hard."

After that conversation, their relationship flourished. Both sexually inexperienced they understood one another. "Practice makes perfect," Sarah would joke. Or was she joking? They behaved as if they were going for a gold medal in the sex Olympics. They blushed together as they intently watched sexually-explicit movies. They ordered and referred to *The Guide to Getting It On* by Paul Joannides, they tagged Kamasutra.org and Wewomen.com's Kamasutra sex position website pages on Sarah's laptop computer. Practices were frequent and intense, often leaving them spent and in need of electrolyte replenishment. "We should do a Gatorade commercial," Tony would joke.

It didn't take long before naive and quiet polite conversations and childish teasing were replaced with heat, seductive glances, intimate secrets, and the touching, those caresses that seem to happen accidentally while riding in a crowded elevator, they were anything but accidental—in fact, they were quite intentional.

For both of them, Monday through Friday had become a means to get to the weekend when they would spend every moment together again. Because Tony stilled lived with his parents, the weekends were spent at Sarah's small apartment, he began leaving a change of clothes, neatly folded on an out-of-the way chair, and when he returned to her apartment on the following Friday night, he found them hanging in the closet next to hers.

Eventually, a single drawer in her bedroom bureau was cleared for Tony, and slowly, he filled it. When his mother, Rosalie, noticed that his laundry basket at home became lighter and lighter, she asked, "So, Tony Junior, we'owr all ya clothes? Yower hampa is empty. I don see any uv ya pants? Don't tell me that yo finally takin yo shirts to da dry cleanas." He just shrugged. She'd never understand that her baby boy was growing up.

One afternoon, as he and Sarah were walking through the botanical gardens at Golden Gate Park, Tony seemed unusually quiet. Sarah knew that he had been struggling with something for a few weeks. She just didn't know what it was, but was hopeful that Tony would talk about it when he was ready. When he took Sarah's hand in his and led her toward a bench, she knew that something was wrong. Raised by a Jewish mother, Sarah knew doom was always around the corner. She took a deep breath to steel herself.

"Sarah, sit down. I really have to tell you something." He seemed uneasy. He could hardly look her in the eye.

She stopped. *Oh no.* Her heart began to break and tears formed in her eyes. "Are you going to break up with me? Did you find someone else? Is that what's been on your mind?" She looked away as she wiped her tears with the sleeve of her sweater. "I knew it."

"Oh no, Sarah. It's not that." This was going to be harder than he thought it would be.

"I should have figured it out." She couldn't hold in the sob. "Have I done something?"

"No, no, you haven't done anything. Please don't cry. I just wanted to tell you that . . ." he swallowed hard. "That, I love you."

"You do?" She had gotten herself so upset that her nose was running and she developed a case of the hiccups.

"Yes, I do and I think that we should consider, maybe . . . perhaps, oh I don't know . . . a future together." He swallowed hard. "What do you think?"

"I don't know, Tony." She hiccupped. "What do I think of what?"

Tony realized that he wasn't being as articulate as he had planned to be, and Sarah was not following his line of thought. So, he reached into his pocket and pulled out a small velvet box and snapped it open to reveal a sweet little ring. Then he cleared his throat and asked, "Sarah, what do you think of marrying me?"

Four weeks later, a very nervous Tony and his equally nervous fiancé decided to bring their families together for a brunch to meet and become acquainted. It was time. They had been dating for over two years and although he had met Sarah's family and Sarah had spent time with Tony's family as well, now that they were planning their future together, it meant that the two very overbearing, overly protective, and the no-one-is-good-enough-for-my-(fill in the blank) mothers would have to meet.

Judith and Jules Weinberg arrived first. Jules' hand was nearly chopped off by the spinning doors as Judith excitedly pushed through ahead of him. "I'm kvelling. I'm kvelling." She beamed as she raced through the lobby. "I have such *knochis,* my heart might burst from happiness. Where is she? Where is she? Where's the bride?" When she reached her daughter, she held Sarah's face in her hands and kissed her five or six times. "I've waited so long for this day." She looked around. "Where's my son-in-law to be?" She took a breath and placed her hand on her bosom, "Jules, Jules dahlink, would you get me a glass of water? I think I might faint."

"I'm behind you, Mrs. Weinberg." Tony smiled shyly and waved his hand hoping to avoid a kiss-attack.

"Oh, Tony, honey," Judith grabbed him by the face and kissed him. "We're going to have to work on the Mrs. Weinberg thing. Mrs. Weinberg is my mother-in-law and believe me, one Mrs. Weinberg is enough for a lifetime." She gazed over at her husband and rolled her eyes. "God help us all." Turning back to Tony Jr., she instructed him, "I want you to call me Judith, or better yet, call me mom."

She turned back to Sarah, "Where is the *mishpucha*?"

"The what?" Tony asked.

"*Mishpucha*! You know, 'the family.'" Not understanding Yiddish is just one of the downfalls of marrying a *shaygetz*. "Your parents, Tony. Your parents. *Mishpucha*!" She explained. Judith was a little miffed. As it was, she always liked to make an entrance, yet Tony's parents weren't there to see it. "Tony, honey, where are your parents? Are they usually late?"

Just then, the revolving doors started moving, and Rosalie's voice preceded her. "Come on, Anthony. I hate being late. It's just rude. Do you want them to think were *maleducato*?"

"Mom. Dad," Tony walked up and kissed his mother. "No, they won't think you're impolite. They just got here too." Tony Jr. kissed his father Tony Sr.

"They're late?" Rosalie huffed under her breath. "What kinda people come late to their daughter's brunch? What kinda manners is that?" Rosalie didn't comprehend how comical her double standard was.

"Everyone is late." Tony tried to make a joke. He led his parents over to a lobby's main sitting area where the Weinbergs were waiting. When Tony and Sarah made the introductions, Judith and Rosalie exchanged air-kisses then looked each other up and down to size up her competition. This in-law ritual was reminiscent of the Sharks and Jets right before they broke into the Westside Story rumble song and dance routine to "Tonight."

"The maître d' said he'll come and get us when our table is ready. In the mean time, we have a bottle of Prosecco for a toast." Tony started to pour it into the glasses.

"Oh, what a beautiful blouse," Judith offered and reached to feel the fabric of Rosalie's top. "They can do such wonderful things with synthetics nowadays. You're lucky. I need to wear breathable, organic materials and they tend to be more expensive. Sure," she nodded and looked again at Rosalie's blouse, "comfort is important, but *I* like to be fashionable. What can I say?" she shrugged. "*I* care about what other people think."

"Well, Judith," Rosalie snapped back. "Can I say that yours is a beautiful hair color? My friend Lorraine does hers at home too and loves the bold off-colors also." *Take that!* Rosalie was no slouch at serving up her own back-handed compliment.

Jules and Anthony Sr. both sat back and settled into the lobby sofas. They had more in common than they knew. Both had outspoken wives, and both chose to simply be in attendance and not even attempt to speak. And both independently had decided that the wives would just have to suit up and work out their differences in the in-law-Thunderdome.

"Mom, dad, listen, I wanted to tell you something." Tony Jr. turned to his parents. "I'm going to move into Sarah's apartment, now, before the wedding. I'll help with the bills and it gives us a chance to get used to being with one another."

"What is this getting used to stuff?" Judith asked. "This is not a sweater that you can return the store because it doesn't fit right. Grandma and grandpa were fixed up by a *yenta*. Do you think they had a breaking-in period? No. They just made it work. I'm telling you, Rosalie," She looked at her future in-laws, "kids today."

"Anthony, honey, aren't you happy at home? Have I done something to drive you away?" Rosalie couldn't fathom the idea that Tony Jr. wouldn't want to be with his own mother for as long as possible. "Your father and I lived with his parents for the first three years of our marriage. We only moved because Pops needed one of those big, mechanical, hospital-type beds. It was too big to take upstairs, so we had to put it in the living room. Then you were born and there just wasn't enough room anymore. Otherwise, who knows, we might still be there today. Isn't that right, Tony?" Rosalie slapped her husband's arm.

"They're dead now, Ro," Tony Sr. answered, exasperated.

"You?" Rosalie looked at Judith. "You let your daughter live alone in the city?"

"Listen Rosalie, it's not a question of 'let' anymore. These kids, they graduate college, they get a job, a little money," she shrugged, "and next thing you know they're smarter than everyone."

"Well, Tony Jr.," Rosalie turned to her son, "Does she make a good sauce?" She nodded at Sarah.

"Sauce?" Sarah asked.

"Yeah, sauce," Rosalie knew Sarah, who was not Italian, might not know the importance of "sauce," so she elaborated. "Sauce . . . Sunday Gravy? You know, marinara. Ragu?" She rolled her eyes.

"Well . . . no. I mean, not yet. We," she looked at Tony, "thought we would learn to cook together."

"You'll starve." Rosalie shook her head and laughed as she sat back.

"Oy!" Judith laughed. She and Rosalie smiled at one another. "I don't think Jules even knows where our kitchen is."

"Oh yeah, the last time my Tony was in the kitchen, he nearly cut off his own thumb making a sandwich."

"Here's what we'll do," Rosalie scooted forward and spoke directly to Sarah, "You'll come over tada house on Sundays and we'll cook. I'll teach you sauce, red sauce, a bolognese, a ragu, and a white sauce." She started counting out the dishes on her fingers as she listed them. "Macaroni, cutlets, meatballs, parmigiana—you know, the basics. Aftawads, fish, salumi, and so on..."

"And, on Saturdays," Judith chimed in. She was desperate to mark her territory, make herself a vital cog in the planning of Tony and Sarah's lives. "*We* will shop and plan the wedding. And after that, God willing, we'll plan for the baby."

"From your lips to Gods ears, Judith." Rosalie placed the palms of her hands together and looked upwards, she repeated "From your lips . . ."

The baby! Tony Jr. and Sarah looked at each other wide eyed. They had barely made it past finding closet space for

Tony's things. The baby discussion was a bit premature. "Just be happy they're getting along," Tony whispered.

"First things first, Rosalie," Judith said as she put her hand on Rosalie's. "The holidays." Rosalie nodded, indicating that this was an issue for her as well. "How are we going to handle the holidays?"

"Yes, let's get this out on the table now and figya it out. I think that's smart to do it early on," Rosalie agreed whole-heatedly.

"I don't think people do . . . and then there are problems." Judith nodded.

"Well Christmas and Easta', those are no-brainas. Since you're Jewish, we'll do it at awwa house."

"Just as a mention," Judith added, "We'll have to talk if Passover happens on Easter. It's different every year."

"What's with you people? Can't you choose a date and keep with it?" Using her hands, one then the other, she emphasized, "This holiday happens on the third Tuesday after a full moon. That holiday is a hop, skip, and a jump afta the first rainy day. I won't be able to keep track." Rosalie threw her hands up.

"I'll help you. So I think we can agree that Hanukkah is ours." Judith made the statement.

"Is it Hanukkah with an H or is it Cha-nu-kah with a cha? Who knows? Can't you people commit?"

"Listen," Rosalie, thought she was revealing the elephant in the room. "We're really gonna havta figya out the Thanksgiving. For twenty-three years," she stated her case, "I always have the whole familia, brothers, and sisters and nieces and nephews and all of their fambolies. Lasagna, veal, sometimes turkey, tortellini, roasted pumpkin soup, lamb, roasted potatoes . . . Then I have a tiramisu or a crostata, some gelato, and always expresso. Always." She emphasized. "It's a wonderful time. Ask anyone."

"Yes, but we have a tradition too." Judith plead her case for Thanksgiving. "We go to the Four Seasons for their buffet. You know, *they* say . . . it's the best Thanksgiving in the city. It's written up in all of the magazines."

"Wait a minute. Hold the phone." Rosalie couldn't believe her ears. "You don't-a cook?" "What kinda motha don't cook?"

Sarah and Tony sat there, eyes opening wide after the last exchange. It was one thing listening to their mothers plan out their lives, but it looked as though there might be some fisticuffs over where they were going to eat turkey and mashed potatoes.

Sensing that his wife Rosalie was going to start something unpleasant, Tony Sr. jumped into the conversation. "You know what? This may be too much for one day."

"Yes," Jules agreed. "You ladies should get a calendar, sit down with a cup-a-coffee, and a nice piece-a-cake and negotiate. The kids," he nodded at Tony and Sarah, "should also have some input and that way everyone knows what's what."

"Agreed!" Tony Sr. pounded the table with his hand and ended the conversation. "Today is a day of celebration, and that's what we're gonna do." He raised his glass of Prosecco. "To da kids."

"Yes, the kids. Mazel tov. *Zie ga zink!*" Judith raised her glass and clinked it against Rosalie's. Looking at each other, it was unspoken but clear. The discussion about the holidays was far from over.

"So kids," Rosalie broke from Judith's glare, and asked, "Why're ya so quiet?"

"You'll excuse me for interrupting," Oscar Pasternak had walked up and was now standing over the families, "but I had to come over and say congratulations."

Judith dramatically grasped her chest. "Oh my Got!"

Rosalie screamed at the top of her lungs, "Ahh! You're Whatshisname, right?"

Oscar smiled. He loved being recognized, however he wished that his fans fell more into the twenty-to-thirty year old category rather than fifty and above. But he took what he could get. "Yes, I'm Oscar Pasternak." He bowed.

Rosalie smacked Tony Sr. "Why can't you be gallant like that?"

"Wha? You want me to bow to you now? Yo nuts, Ro." He waved her off.

"I wanted to say that this scene reminds me of a Metro picture I did with the talented Miss Tovah Feldshuh back in the eighties. She played a young Jewess, a musician from Israel, and I played an Irish soldier." He set the scene. "The odds were against us," he explained, "but I won over her parents by saving the grandmother from the Nazis." He looked at the group, "Have you seen it? It was called *Rivka O'Malley*. It was really the *Titanic* of its day." He looked at Jules and Tony Sr. "That Tovah, she was a pistol." He smiled. "I should give her a call."

Judith stood up and tossed her Canon SureShot at her husband. "Jules, take a picture of Rosalie and me with Mr. Pasternak to commemorate this occasion."

2:00 P.M.

At 2:00 p.m. sharp, Francis Laporte took his post at the front desk. His name was Francis—not Frank, not Frankie, not Buddy. It was Francis. Fastidious, professional, well read, well-mannered, and well groomed, he was perfect for the job. Unfortunately, he had absolutely no sense of humor. He was extremely literal and very, very serious. He never joked or participated in light conversation with coworkers. For that, his coworkers chided him constantly.

He had studied and was multi-degreed in English literature and the classics, but his degree did not prepare him for any career, other than intellectual snob. Unfortunately, there were very few job listings for poetasters or professional, uptight, elitist smarty-pants. Jobs in marketing or as a copywriter or editorial assistant were all-too-pedestrian for him. He felt his reputation as a true author, a writer of classical literature, would be damaged or at the very least compromised if he lowered himself to write "copy" or tag lines for laundry detergent or feminine hygiene products or two paragraph blurbs about the city's new traffic light at the intersection of Mundane and Trivial. Instead he took a job at the hotel to pay the bills while he worked on his great novel. Convinced that it would be a classic or at the very least on the required reading list, he had been working on it for the past six years.

But he was reliable, focused, chronically polite, smart, and prompt and was willing to work for an hourly wage.

As she did every day during the shift change, Barbara transferred the information about concerns, hi-maintenance guests, and the events planned or unplanned to the next shift's workers. She gathered the afternoon first line reception staff: Victoria "Vicky" Purdue, Constance "Connie" Simons, Charles "Charlie the Trainee" Carmichael, and Francis "Francis" LaPorte.

She looked at her list and read through it. "Keep an eye on the petty cash drawer, it seems light. We have a Chinese tour group arriving around five o'clock. I think there are twenty-five people in the group. I've scheduled Heidi Ho to be here. She speaks Mandarin and will take the lead with these guests. She also offered to stay as late as necessary, if plane is delayed. So you don't have to worry. Tonight we have a class reunion starting at eight. Marisol from housekeeping and Rick from maintenance were at it in the fourth floor linen closet again. They've been counseled, so I don't expect any problems, but let me know if you hear anything." She looked at her clip board. "Let's see. The ice maker on the seventh floor is making noise again. We have a maintenance man working on it now. Vicky, would you check up on it in about a half-hour? Guests in rooms 214, 707, 1122, and 1724 have asked for a late checkout and, finally, there is an employee potluck in the lunch room. Do you have any questions for me?"

"No questions." Vicky spoke up, "I think we have it. Thanks."

"Then that's it. Have a good shift." She looked up and saw woman who was clearly intoxicated staggering toward the reception desk. "Francis, you're up." She smirked. "I'm just going to get my purse and then I'm gone. Good luck."

A woman who was clearly sloshed planted her elbows on the counter and cradled her head in her hands. "Hi ya," she offered a drunken grin.

"Good afternoon, ma'am, may I help you?" Always the professional, Francis tried to overlook her condition.

"Yes, yes you can." She slurred. "I am here to check in. I got here oh, I dunno, 'bout noon o'clock. But the lady," she cut her eyes at Barbara, "wouldn't let me check in. She said that the check in time was at three or four or five or six or sumptin. So I went to the bar and your bartender Maximum made me a few special Coppolomians or sumpthin. They were dee-licious!"

"Maxim," Francis politely corrected her. "The bartender's name is Maxim."

"That's what I said. Maximum. He's very nice." Suddenly Yvonne's face was hanging, as if the muscles simply had given up and her eyes started blinking in slow motion.

Francis realized that it wouldn't be responsible to continue ignoring her condition. He knew that he needed to get this very drunk lady to her room and lying down before she passed out or fell down or worse. "Alright then, let me see how I can help you. What is your name please?"

"My name isn't 'please.' My name is Yvonne. Wuz yer name?"

He tapped his name badge. "It's Francis, ma'am."

"Well Francis Ma'am, I'm Yvonne and I wanna go to my room."

"Yvonne, what is your last name please?" He smiled pleasantly.

"My last name is Addams. That's with two Ds." She paused. "Tutti frutti. Ha! I never thought of that before. I'm Yvonne Tutti-Frutti. Look me up." She pointed at the computer. "Go ahead."

"Although our regular check in time is three o'clock, I will be happy to see if your room is ready now, Miss Addams. One moment please." The screen on his computer said the status of the room had not been changed from "Empty" to "Ready," so he picked up the phone and dialed the house-keeping manager. He intended to ask her to make the room a priority. While he did, Yvonne crossed her arms on the counter and rested her head.

Yvonne reeked of alcohol and had just developed a case of the hiccups. Not the dry, cute, whoopsy, oh-my-goodness hiccup-y type of hiccups, but the air-gulping, body-jolting, gurgling hors d'oeuvres before the main coarse type of hiccups.

As if someone poked her, her head popped up and she started talking again. "I am here for my stepsister's wedding, you know. I am older and prettier than her, yet she's the one getting married. Go figure." Yvonne shrugged her shoulders and threw her hands up. "I think it's because she has big tits. They're like double Qs. I don't know how she keeps from falling over." She pulled the collar of her blouse out in front of her and looked down her own blouse. "Mine aren't so bad. Don't you think?"

"I think all of the time, ma'am."

"Always the bridesmaid . . ." she continued. "You know, I had a boyfriend, but he broke up with me. After two years, he said, he said, he said that he fell in love with someone else. Could you believe that?" Yvonne made a "pfft" sound and waved her hand.

Francis didn't look up. "I'm sure you will make a beautiful bridesmaid, Miss Addams."

"But whadda ya gonna do? Say 'go un-fall in love with her' or 'go un-meet her?' No." She shook her head hard and then thought for a moment. "Well, you know what they say . . ." It was more a statement than a question. "If you love someone, then set him free . . . And hope that he gets crushed by a falling tree." She laughed a little then her expression turned sad.

After a few seconds she snapped out of it. "Anyway . . ." Yvonne squinted at Francis' name tag. "Francis?" she said. "That's a girl's name, isn't it?"

With the receiver to his ear, he answered the question he had heard a million times before. "Sometimes, ma'am. And sometimes Francis is a man's name." He held up his finger hoping to quiet her as he listened to the voice on the other end of the extension. "I see," he said. "Well this guest needs to lie down *right now*. And if the room is not ready immediately, I may be calling you to clean up something very unpleasant in the lobby, if you understand what I am saying." He listened again. "Okay, wonderful. Thank you very much Miss Sophia."

As he hung up the receiver he said, "Good news Miss Addams. Your room will be ready by the time you get up there." He printed the key card. "Now, do you have any luggage?"

She looked around her and suddenly appeared worried. "Where are my bags? Someone has stolen my bags." Then she shouted, "call the police!" and fell against the counter again.

"Miss Addams," he tried to calm and quiet her. "Is it possible that when you got here at noon you left the bags with the bellman to hold until your room was ready?"

Exaggeratedly she nodded. "Yes. That's 'zactly what happened. You are like Sherlock Holmes. Maybe I should call you 'Shirley' instead of Francis."

Francis was losing his patience. "Miss Addams, I can see that you want to get to your room right away. So I will have your bags sent up after you, and I will get your credit card information a little later." He looked around the lobby and waved over a female security guard. Francis handed her the key and told her the room number.

"Miss Addams, this is Brenda and she will escort you and make sure you get to your room safe and sound. And, if it's alright," he continued. "I'll have her check up on you in an hour to make sure you're feeling okay." He nodded at Brenda.

She looked at the brawny security guard. "Hi there, you're a big one, aren't cha? Waz yer name?"

She took her elbow and started leading her away from the desk, "My name is Brenda, ma'am."

"Well Brenda Ma'am, lead the way."

As they stumbled toward to the elevators, Yvonne asked, "Could you wake me up in time for the bachelorette party?" She had another thought. "Brenda Ma'am? Are you related to Francis Ma'am?"

"Nice work, Francis Ma'am," Connie smirked as she adjusted the security monitor screen. "I'm not sure I would have had as much patience with her."

Francis just shrugged. He noticed their next early check-in and looked over at Connie, "I think this one is yours."

Connie followed Francis' eyes and saw a throwback from the disco-era swaggering toward her. At first glance she thought he was naked, but as he approached, she realized that he was dressed all in beige. Not a pleasant, soothing, subtle beige, but a yellowy-orange, baby puke beige, head to toe, turtle neck down to polyester bell bottoms. The naked effect was only interrupted by a white belt and a pair of scuffed white disco boots.

"Hey there, little lady," he pointed his index fingers at her, making finger pistols. "How are you doing today?" He winked. He looked over at Charlie the trainee, "How's it hangin', dude?" Charlie finger pistoled him back.

He looked at Connie's badge. "Constance huh? Hey baby," he cooed, "that's such a serious name for such a hot lady. Listen, sugar, I know I'm a little early but I'm hoping you can check me in. I'd like to get in a little disco-nap before the big class reunion tonight." He put one elbow on the desk, and eyed her over his shoulder. He had positioned himself so everyone in the lobby could get a good look at him, *Yup, take it all in, ladies.* His greying pompadour-slash-mullet and puffy *Magnum P.I.* mustache were only the beginning. Connie could imagine that this gum-chewing guy who clearly peaked in high school had pulled up to the hotel in his old Dodge Dart with a *Dukes of Hazzard* paint job. While he was turned away nodding at all of the women in the lobby, she looked him over again. Her eyes rested on his pleather belt. *Whats that?* Instead of a cellphone or a pager or even an insulin pump, he had a garage door opener. Connie looked back at the security monitor hoping that the camera caught a picture of this guy. Without proof, no one would ever believe her description of this clown.

"Let's see what we can do." She positioned her fingers over the keyboard. "What is your name, please?"

"I'm Lance, Lance Cochran. But my friends call me Lance Shall-we-dance, In-your-pants Cochran." He said it while doing an Elvis pelvis move. When he was done he finger pistoled her again.

Connie threw up a little in her mouth. *What a douche bag!* "Well Mr. Cockring . . ."

He corrected her. "That's Cochran, babydoll."

"Here it is." Connie looked at the computer screen and smiled. "We have an Economy Queen for you, and it appears to be ready." She began printing his card key. "How many keys will you need?"

"Just one, darlin'. I couldn't decide which chicky to bring, so to be fair, I didn't bring any of them. This way, I'm open to all of the possibilities the night might bring. But," he winked, "you can make an extra one for yourself if you like what you see." He stepped back then held his arms out to the side.

If she had rolled her eyes as much had she wanted to, she would have looked like she was having a seizure and the paramedics would have been called in. "No thank you, Mr. Cochran. May I have a credit card for extras? As you know, nothing will be charged unless you use the minibar or charge purchases to you room."

"Honey, I believe I can get a company discount. Ya wanna check?" He leaned in. "Check under Interstate Bakery Corporation, you know, Hostess Cupcakes. *Sweet* job." He chuckled at his own joke. Lance had worked as a driver, delivering cupcakes and Twinkies and Wonder Bread to gas stations and convenience stores since he got the job directly after high school, twenty-five years earlier. "Hey baby, what kind of cake do you like?" He licked his lips and winked.

"Carrot, sir." *Oh crap*, in an attempt to shut him down, she realized that she opened herself up for another disgusting double entendre. Her pithiness was no match for this oozing pile of lewdness, so she tried to keep it from happening. "Here we go, sir. Your corporate discount will appear on your final bill." She placed his key on the counter. "You're in room 201, right next to the elevators and ice machine. Enjoy your stay."

"Oh, I intend to, Constance. Hey, I have a little sumptin' sumptin' for you." He reached into his bag and pulled out a package of pink Hostess Snowballs and slid them across the counter. "There's more of that where that came from." He blew her a kiss then picked up his bag.

As he walked away, Connie mumbled, "Thank you, sir." More than anything, she wanted to be offended and disgusted. But the truth was, she loved Hostess Snowballs.

◆ ◆

Charlie, the trainee, seemed to be in a trace. He was staring out into the lobby. "Who is that?" He whispered.

"Who, Charlie?" Connie followed his eyes and there stood a beautiful young woman. She was small and delicate. Her fine, blond hair was long and pulled back into a pony-tail, making her look younger than she was. She was wearing a bellman's jacket and struggling while trying to move a luggage cart. "Oh, that's Jenny. She's new. The management said something about equal opportunity and hired an eighty-nine pound pixie to haul luggage."

"Oh, um hum," Charlie was hardly listening. He was entranced.

"Vicky," Connie whispered in her ear, "I think our young Charlie, has a crush."

"No, no I don't," Charlie cleared his throat. "I was just wondering . . ."

Just then, there was a loud crashing sound coming from across the lobby. Jenny was standing over a fallen luggage cart, several pieces of luggage were on the floor, and poor Jenny stood there with her hands covering her ears.

"I'll be right back," Charlie told Vicky who answered, "No you won't. You're not going over there."

"What are you talking about? I should help her."

Vicky smiled at Connie. They were going have to educate Charlie. "Charlie, honey," she started, "what you need to understand is that helping Jenny with her job would be a monumentally bad idea."

"Especially if you want to get into her pants," Connie interjected.

"Little Miss Tiny-Pants over there took this job to prove a point. Don't you think she knows that she's the size of a fairy with all the strength of an infant?"

"Of course she does," Connie picked up the tag. "And if you help her, you're telling her that you don't think she can do her job, and you'll embarrass her in front of the other bellmen. And then you know what happens then?"

In harmony both Connie and Vicky answered, "She'll hate you."

"But it looks like she's crying . . ." Charlie had a pleading in his voice.

"Stop staring at her. There will be another opportunity to meet her." Vicky assured him. "Who knows, she may come over here to meet you."

3:00 P.M.

Three o'clock is check-in time. It's the staff's second least favorite time for the day, second only to noontime checkout. As they readied themselves for the new guests to arrive, they hope that the room status is correct on the computer, the housekeeping staff had finished servicing the rooms, and there weren't any stragglers, late checkouts, or unmade beds. The front desk clerks hated to get *that* call—the call from a new guest ranting that his room is dirty or that someone was already in it.

Vicky stood behind the counter waiting to see who would either rush the desk or try to look nonchalant as they checked in exactly at 3:00 p.m. on the dot. Those were the anxious guests who refused to miss even one minute of their reservation. It usually meant trouble.

She had noticed a small group of travelers who were already inebriated when they arrived two hours earlier and then waited in the bar until check-in time. Their clothes looked as if they dressed with the intention of looking messy. Worn-out rock 'n' roll types—not KISS or Bruce Springstein rock 'n' roll, but a group of forty-plus-year-old guys who set up their "equipment" in someone's mom's garage and talked about what could have been while they drank beer and entertained themselves until the neighbors complained. *That kind of rock 'n' roll.*

"Oh shit, here they come." Victoria said to Charlie as they stood behind the counter. "Ten bucks they come to me. I always attract those types. Never a 'please' or 'thank you,' just a bunch gross flirting and obnoxious demands." Vicky tried not to stare at the band of mouth-breathers as they approached her. She looked down at the desk and pretended to take some notes.

One puffy, pasty, pudgy, balding mess of a man approached, planted his feet, cleared his throat, and began snapping his fingers in front of Vicky's face to get her attention "Hello. Hello. Earth to whatever your name is. I'm checking in here." He glanced back at his sycophants and snickered.

"Victoria. My name is Victoria Purdue." She finished writing her note and looked up. "Are you checking in, sir?" Vicky wasn't going to buy into his behavior.

"Do you know who I am?" A question that is only asked by has-beens and wanna-bes, and shouted by D-, E-, F-, and Q-list asshole celebrities and celebutantes, like Paris Hilton or any of the Kardashians. This one was flanked by the Apple Dumpling Gang of entourages.

"I," he stepped back and held out his arms, "am Double D."

Vicky was not amused, but careful to be on the right side of pleasant verses snarky. "Oh Mr. D., it's nice to meet you. I would be happy to assist you. However, I do not see a reservation for a Double D. Perhaps it's under another name. I will need your full name, please."

It was clear to Double D that Vicky was not only unimpressed and was not making a fuss about his presence in the hotel lobby, but she in fact didn't seem to know who he was. To her, Double D was just like any other guest except he was a little more obnoxious.

"Come on, you know me," He nodded and stood back. "Double D. From TV?" Vicky looked at him blankly. When he realized that his "cred" was getting him nowhere, he leaned in and whispered, "It's under Dingleman."

Double D was the forty-year-old Dennis Dingleman who had appeared briefly on a 1990s teenage angst-centric evening series by Aaron Spelling. Dennis was known to be so untalented and obnoxious that his character was actually killed in a disfiguring car crash in the late episodes of the show's first season. Having Double D's character transfer high schools and move out of town was not enough for the producers. They wanted to preclude any chance of Dennis ever coming back to the show, even for a visit. Not only did the writers kill off the character, they also left him mangled and unrecognizable. So if there was ever a dream sequence or flashback, the show could cast someone else in his place.

It's pretty difficult to be thrown off of an ensemble cast of amateurish teenagers whose only talents are to pose, pout, and deny having plastic surgery. Yet his behavior warranted it. Double D was never invited back to any retrospective or reunion shows and his name was removed from fan websites and the Internet Movie Database.

Since his reputation preceded him to auditions, it was nearly impossible for him to secure other television roles. Lacking any other skills, he made his way around the has-been circuit: *Stomping with the Stars*, *Celebrity Chefs on Ice*, and *Pimp My Rented-Studio-Apartment-Crib in Reseda*. He was so desperate for publicity, that in a last-ditch effort for attention, he intentionally gained sixty pounds so he could appear on *Celebrity Fit Club*. Unfortunately, he was not selected for the program, and more unfortunately, the diet of fast food and alcohol that he used to gain the sixty pounds resulted in acne, girl hips, and ironically, Double D now sported a set of moobs.

Being obnoxious and untalented was a double whammy for Dennis. Having one of those traits is tolerable, but having *both* presented impossible hurdles to overcome for anyone unless he or she was astonishingly beautiful, extremely rich, had a parent who was a celebrity, or had close ties in the Hollywood community.

In fact, the only thing that Dennis was known for these days was his misbehavior. He was regularly cited for drunk driving, lewd and disruptive behavior, destruction of property, and theft. Rather than admit any wrong doing, like so many other fallen celebrities, his attorney labeled his unbearable conduct an "addiction," an "-ism," and whenever jail time was threatened he would "voluntarily" check himself into rehab for twenty-eight day stints. And why not? Mel Gibson went to rehab for being a bigoted asshole, any number of wife beating, drug addled immature and entitled sports figures checked-in, and various child stars practically lived in rehab as a result of having bad parents or over-inflated egos, or both. Why not Double D for Obnoxious-ism?

More recently, he had pitched a reality show idea to the Bravo network. The premise was that cameras would follow him as he tried to break into the porn industry. The project, considered provocative at first, was scrapped during the initial planning stage when multiple porn directors determined that Double D's poor acting skills would distract from the story lines.

Standing at the registration desk, Double D barked at Charlie who was standing next to Vicky. "Yo! You! Do you have any bottled water? I'm dyin' of thirst here."

When Charlie handed a bottle to him, he grabbed it and sarcastically said, "I meant a bottle of *cold* water. I didn't realize that I had to be so 'pacific' . . . duh!"

"Yeah," He continued. His voice loud enough for anyone within twenty feet of him to hear. "I'm here in town to do a sort of 'where are they now' slash real estate investment infomercial. Not really my type of gig, but the director's a friend of mine and you know how it is. I'm doing him a solid." It was all big talk from Double D. Deep inside he knew the "where are they now" slant would portray him as a loser of epic proportions. But he needed the money and was desperate for the exposure. Besides, Dennis agreed with P.T. Barnum: "There is no such thing as bad publicity."

"Yes, sir, Dennis Dingleman. Here we are." Vicky announced loudly. "A queen size, economy room made through Priceline. I see that you have requested three roll away beds." Vicky made an affected frowny face. "I'm sorry sir, fire laws prohibit more than one rollaway bed in a room that size. However, if you would like to upgrade to a suite. Your entire . . ."

"Entourage," Double D clarified.

"Yes, sir, your entourage," Vicky wanted to roll her eyes, "could sleep comfortably. The suite is appointed with a king size bed, a fold out couch, and a sleeping chair, plus there is room for two additional roll away beds . . ."

He leaned over the desk and whispered, "How much coin would that set me back?"

"Yes, Mr. Dingleman, that would be $1,525 a night, plus tax."

Knowing that the $269 deal he received was over his budget to begin with, $1,500 was completely out of the question. To save face, he laughed loudly. "Hell no," he turned around and said to his people. "That's okay 'cuz we're gonna be out partying all night." This announcement was followed by a smattering of fake "woo hoos" and fist pumping from his limp entourage.

"Okay, sir, good for you." Vicky pulled a piece of paper off the printer and set it on the counter. "All I need is a credit card for room expenses and you're set."

"A credit card? Wha—! You're kidding, right?" He laughed at her. "No. *You* comp *me* for choosing to stay here. What you get in return is free publicity. *That* is the way it is done."

Jackass. "Oh, sir, I'm sorry, that should have been arranged prior to your arrival." She laughed to herself. This guy's self-importance was comical. She decided to play with him. "I can, however, offer you two complimentary breakfast buffets in the cafe." She handed him two coupons, each worth a few bucks.

Looking at the coupons in his hand, he seemed confused. He held his hands out toward her. "But there are six of us."

"Sir, I am only authorized . . ." she looked at his dumb face and suddenly felt sorry for him. He was desperately trying to appear important. All he wanted was for someone to notice him and make even the smallest fuss over him. As she stood there, Vicky realized how sad the situation was. She wondered, *When did I get so tainted, so cruel? A few free breakfasts wouldn't bankrupt the hotel. The mark up is about 300%, anyway. Oh hell.* "Wait a minute, sir." She held out her hand. "Give those back to me, please."

"No, that's okay." He pulled them back to his chest. "I didn't mean to sound ungrateful, really. Two is fine."

"No, it's not. Hold on." Vicky opened a few drawers and found what she was looking for. She grabbed six Deluxe Brunch Certificates. "Here you go, sir." If you'd like to use them this weekend, I will be happy to make a reservation for you and your . . ." She smiled, "group."

He thanked her quietly. Then as he turned around, he held the tickets in the air. "Score!" he yelled and pumped his fist. "Thanks, doll." He said over his shoulder and strutted back to his group—uh, his entourage. "You see, I've still got it. *This* is gonna be a great trip."

Connie had walked up just as Vicky was handing Dennis the six tickets. As she placed some fresh apples in the decorative bowl on the counter, she wanted to know. "Who was that? Why did you give him those brunch tickets?"

"Oh," Charlie snickered. "He's a huge nobody?" Charlie shook his head, "*That's* who he is."

"Exactly," Vicky smiled. "That's exactly why I gave him the brunch tickets."

Vicky straightened her jacket and looked out into the lobby awaiting their next guest.

A loud woman wearing a louder Hawaiian print cabana set and hideous waterproof sandals walked into the lobby. "There's no way we're paying those prices for valet parking! What is it? Forty bucks a day? Then you have to tip the guy too!" Reminiscent of the character George Kellerman in 1970s film *The Out of Towners*, Darlene Wilkerson thought everyone was out to cheat her. But *she* was no patsy, and she was *not* going to be taken advantage of.

"You know it's all a scam, don't you?" Darlene said loud enough for everyone in the lobby to hear. "First there's the guy who opens the car door. You have to tip him. Then it's the guy who pulls the luggage out of the trunk. Then, it's the guy who parks the car. Where does it end?" Embarrassed, her henpecked husband Brad shook his head and looked apologetically at Jacqueline, a small, older woman who had just entered the lobby and was walking toward the desk to check-in.

"What now?" She addressed her husband. "Did your father die and leave us a big inheritance that I don't know about? Did you win the lottery? Hmm?" Darlene looked around. "Where are Darren and Darcy, anyway? Are they still moping about having to walk from the car? Those kids don't know how good they've got it. We didn't have to bring them. I know we're here because tonight is your high school reunion, but I thought it would be nice to make it into a family vacation."

Brad cleared his throat, "Um, Darren and Darcy are just a few steps behind me with the beach gear." A minute later, sandy-legged and sunburnt eleven-year-old Darren and nine-year-old Darcy schlepped through the lobby struggling with towels, beach chairs, hats, and blow-up rafts.

"Darlene, honey," Brad asked his wife, "is it really necessary to bring it all in? Couldn't we just leave it in the car?"

"Darcy, Darren, leave that man alone." The kids had run over to where Oscar Pasternak was sitting. She turned back to face her husband. "Brad, this isn't downtown Hooterville, 1950. If we leave anything in the car, I'll tell you what . . . It will be gone in the morning. And we're stuck with a bill for repairing the broken windows and out the thirty bucks we paid for those rafts and towels." Then under her breath, but loud enough from Brad to hear, she added, "Money doesn't grow on trees." She glanced at the kids, "Darcy, Darren, damn it! Get over here."

"I think he's dead." Darcy yelled across the lobby. Charlie's snapped his head around and rushed toward Oscar.

"Then for sure, leave him alone." Darlene continued speaking to her husband, "Aren't you glad I suggested stopping at that grocery store? They charge six dollars for a bottle of water here. I got twenty-four for $4.99. That's about twenty-one cents a bottle. Brad, would you get me . . ." She looked around. "For Christ's sake! Didn't you bring any in from the car? Now you'll have to go back and get them. That is, if no one has stolen them by now."

"But honey, the kids want to go to the pool." He looked at his watch. "I was hoping you'd take them and I could go to the bar and use this coupon that came with the 'Reunion' packet." He pulled a card out of his wallet. "Remember? I told you that some old friends from high school are meeting at four o'clock for a drink."

She grabbed the drink coupon from her husband. "You'll see them later. Right now, this is family time and we are all going to the pool . . ." she emphasized, "together."

Appalled by the disrespect and insolence she just witnessed, Jacqueline thought, *Americans treat public venues like it's their own private living room. Where is the decorum? Whatever happened to respect and gentility?* But truthfully, the same displays occurred in Europe too. Should she be so judgmental of Americans, or was she just being French, and conditioned to think that way? Besides, she was in town to visit with her dearest friend May, and May was an American.

As she walked to the front desk, Oscar stood up and bowed. "Hello young lady. It's nice to see you again." Although they were just acquaintances, the hotel staff had informed Oscar that Jacqueline was coming for her annual visit. "My dear, I'm hoping that you will have sometime during your visit to have a glass of wine with me."

"Oh, Mister Pasternak," she smiled and extended her hand to her old friend. "I have to admit. When I looked over here and saw the children poking at you, I thought you may be *mort*, how you say . . . dead."

"Oh no, dear Jacqueline." He looked around then whispered, "Sometimes when I don't want to talk to a guest, I act as if I am asleep. But never for you." He kissed her hand. "Are you here to see May?"

"I am," she smiled, "and I must go freshen up."

Oblivious to everything going on around him, Franklin made his way toward the front desk as if by radar. Franklin Lipnick, hipster-slash-techno-riche-slash-entitled-twerp was focused on his PDA. With his head down, reading the scrolling information passing across the extra large cellphone screen, he stepped forward toward the front desk. Dressed in yellow-colored, tight-legged (yet saggy-assed) pants, leather wingtip shoes without socks, a short-sleeved, fitted, yet un-ironed vintage button-down shirt, horn-rimmed glasses, and a Knit cap, he had a waxed mustache and a goatee. Twenty-four-year old Franklin Lipnick was checking in.

"Ah-hem," Vicky cleared her throat, "May I help you sir."

"Shush." He held up his index finger and shushed her. His fingernail was painted a glossy black. It irritated and amused Vicky at the same time. A minute later, he looked up and gave her a tolerant smile as he placed his phone, boom box, messenger bag, and reusable Jamba Juice cup on the counter and took off his pair of giant headphones. He pulled a vaping stick from his pocket and pointed it at her, "Yes. I'm Lipnick, Franklin Lipnick."

"Okay, thank you, sir." Before she started typing, she nodded toward his smoking device, "No smoking in here, sir."

"But it's a vaping stick," he demanded in a spoiled brat kind of way. "It was designed . . ."

Without looking up she informed him, "No vaping is allowed in the hotel, sir." She continued, "Okay, Mr. Lipnick. We have a regular room with a king-sized bed. And you'll be here through the thirty-first?" She printed his room key, told him his room number, and pointed out the elevator bank. "Is there anything else sir?"

"Yes, there is. I have a number of questions for you." He started, "Is there free Wi-Fi in my room?"

"Yes, sir."

"In the lobby?"

"Yes."

"Is there a place to store my bicycle?"

"Yes."

"Is there an artisanal coffee house within walking distance? Do they have Wi-Fi?"

"Yes, and I don't know."

"A vegan restaurant?"

"Yes, the concierge can make a reservation for you."

"Are you sure it's a vegan restaurant? I didn't say vegetarian or pescaterian," he wagged his finger at her. "I want to be sure you understood what I was asking."

"Yes, sir." She wanted to reach across the counter and slap his mini handlebar mustache off of his face.

"Can I get my room refrigerator filled with coconut water?"

"Yes."

"I need a juicer in my room."

"Okay."

"I have an important brunch appointment tomorrow. Where is your dining room?"

"The dining room is across the lobby, over there," she pointed across the lobby, "and through the double doors."

He smirked, "Then we're cool."

"Thank you, sir." She held out his room key.

"Oh," he stopped, and pulled his hands up close to his chest and looked at her as if she just crawled up from the sewer. He thought for a moment then dug in his messenger bag and handed her a travel-sized bottle of hand sanitizer. "Would you be a doll and use this before handling my room key?" He pointed his vaping stick at her hands. "Thanks so much. There's no telling what you've touched today." He huffed a laugh and gave her a tolerant smile.

Vicky took the hand sanitizer and squeezed some on her hands, and then Franklin Lipnick watched her as she printed a new room key for him. "That's a good girl."

Vicky forced a smile.

"Aren't you going to tell me to have a nice day?" he looked at her name tag, "Vicky?"

"Yes, sir. Oh, one more thing," she pointed across the lobby. "Did you leave your luggage with the bellman?" When Franklin turned to see who Vicky was pointing at, she licked his keycard. "Have a nice day, sir." She handed it to him.

4:00 P.M.

Petite, elegant, and French, Madame Jacqueline Argent was a memorable woman. She had visited the hotel every year since 1959, with the exception of a two-year period in the early 1990s, around the time when her beloved husband Maurice died. After some time passed, she resumed the stateside visits, traveling on her own. "Does the mourning really ever end?" she once asked her dear friend May.

She recalled her many previous trips to the hotel, especially those with Maurice, who had always made her the center of attention, cherishing her as if there were no one else in the room. He was debonair, and so thoughtful. Her simplest wish became his desire; money was no object. Nothing was too good for Jacqueline. She exhaled thoughtfully. She would trade it all in for one more day with him.

The staff remembered and looked forward to her annual visits. Although generations of staff had come and gone over the five decades, Madame and Monsieur Argent's loyal patronage and visits were noted, well known, and as welcomed as Christmas.

Standing less than five feet tall in her sensible heels, the refined Madame Argent wore her thinning dyed-black hair styled in a pageboy cut, a full face of makeup, thick black eyeliner, red lipstick, and the deep, soft wrinkles in her face represented confidence and a life filled with love, experience, and sophistication.

A double strand of large pearls hung from her neck over her smart knit suit with cast gold-plated buttons. One would think that wool in the summer would be too warm, but not for an older woman of elegance. She was bred to remain cool and composed, moving slowly and gracefully even in the most God-awful weather.

Madame Argent walked to the center of the lobby and waited.

Phillippe, the concierge, rushed over to her, took her hand, and kissed the air above it. "Madame Argent. I am so happy to see you again. It has been too long since your last visit," he gushed. "May I assume that you are well, ma'am? How long will we have the pleasure of your presence during this visit to the Shipley?"

"Bonjour, Philippe, I have planned to be here for just one week." She handed him an envelope, "This is for you and your personnel. I want you to know how much Monsieur Argent and I have appreciated your dedication over the years."

He bowed. "How may we be of service to you this afternoon?"

"I would like to entertain my dear friend this afternoon. Would you please set up a small table . . ." she discretely pointed across the lobby to a corner seating area, "there?" She continued, "Missus Bernard will be joining me at half-past four. Philippe, may I ask you to bring a *rafraîchissant*, an aperitif. Perhaps a Lillet or a Dubonnet? I will leave it to you. And one more thing please; if you could, would you find some *petits verres*—uh," she clarified, "small glasses? I see no need to *prendre un bain*, ah . . . take a bath in za enormous American wine glass."

Philippe coordinated his staff who then began scurrying around as they set up the special seating area for Madame

Argent. She was politely seated on the lobby couch, her hands folded in her lap and legs crossed at the ankles. Content to sit and wait for her friend, Jacqueline watched the other guests of the hotel as they moved through their afternoons.

Jacqueline was tired. She had made the 6000 mile trip to see May. Perhaps it was because of her age, her upbringing, or her generation, but there was something that she wanted to tell her friend, and a phone call or even a hand written letter just wouldn't do.

As she waited for her dear May, Jacqueline reminisced. She and Maurice had met May and her husband Jonas in South of France in October of 1956, coincidentally while both couples were on their honeymoons. They became fast friends and together they toured Nice, Cannes, and Saint-Tropez. Jacqueline and May remained in contact throughout the years, mostly through handwritten letters and cards. Initially, they considered each other just as pen pals, but as the years passed, they shared their deep secrets and ideas, discussed dreams, and relied on each other during happy and sad times. Before they knew it, they had become extremely close friends, depending on each other for support and kinship though they were thousands of miles apart.

Jacqueline and her husband Maurice were well off financially and regularly traveled. They made it a point, each time they were in America, to visit May and Jonas and to stay at the Shipley Hotel.

May Bernard and her husband Jonas were a couple of humble means. When Jonas became an airline pilot, it did allow them to travel inexpensively, but his salary provided only enough money for them to live comfortably. As many couples do, they experienced the ups and downs of the economy over the decades, and extravagances were just that—extravagant. During the early years, May wondered why Jacqueline, a woman of elegance and means, would be interested in her friendship, as they led such different lives. But as the years passed, the perceived differences didn't matter. They were confidants, best friends, sisters. May so loved receiving Jaqueline's letters filled with stories of jet-setting and parties and especially looked forward to the annual visits. And Jacqueline waited for May's recipes and photos of her prized garden.

For decades, May would clear her schedule when Jacqueline was in town and take a taxi or bus to the hotel where they would spend leisurely afternoons "catching up."

The doorman opened and held the door for a small, smartly-dressed African-American octogenarian with a laminated bus pass hanging from a lanyard around her neck. She took many, many small shuffling steps. Her forward movement was slow but deliberate. The lady was in no rush. She balanced herself with a carved wooden cane and held her free hand out for assistance from the doorman. She smiled sweetly and stopped to thank and encourage him to "keep up the good work."

Jacqueline recognized her friend. "May, my dear." She stood, smiled kindly, and extended her hands to grasp May's as she toddled over to the seating area. Jacqueline kissed May on both cheeks, "I've missed you."

"I hope I haven't kept you waiting. I'm not as speedy as I used to be," May laughed.

"Oh no, you're right on time. I've been watching the world go by. It's not the same anymore, is it? Gone are the days of dressing for an occasion, *est-ce pas*? I was wondering why it is here in America that people dress as if they are going to clean their garage. But truthfully," she shrugged and shook her head, "I shouldn't be so judgmental of Americans. Alas, it's the same in France."

"It's all about comfort these days." May shrugged. "Since people have these cellular telephones, they never look up or at each other when they have a conversation anyway. Maybe it's not important to make an impression anymore."

Philippe walked over to the ladies. "Excusez-moi mesdames, êtes-vous prêt à être assis?"

"Oui, Philippe, merci. Mrs. Bernard and I are ready."

Philippe had had the staff set up a special table in the quiet corner of the lobby. It was draped with a white linen cloth and topped with a tiny lamp and small vase holding a single flower. Small plates with decoratively folded tea napkins were set on the table in front of the two small, antique walnut button-back chairs, which were the perfect size for two sophisticated yet shrinking-in-stature women. The chairs were placed next to one another, rather than across from each other, creating an intimate space for the two old friends. Philippe and a waiter manned the seat backs and assisted the women as they sat down. Another waiter brought a tray with two glasses of Lillet and a plate of chocolates sent by the chef. "Voila, deux verres de Lillet et du chef pâtissier une assiette de chocolats." Philippe smiled and straightened up. "Now, if you wish for anything else, please let us know."

"I brought a gift for you, May." Jacqueline unlatched and reached into her purse to pull out an envelope then handed it to her old friend.

May opened the envelope as carefully as if she were disarming a bomb. When she pulled out the contents and she looked at it and raised her hand to modestly cover her smile. "Oh Jacqueline, I nearly forgot about this. This," she pointed at the photo, "is when we first met. Wasn't it 1956?" The black-and-white photo showed both May and Jacqueline, then eighteen and nineteen years old, looking stylish as they both sat atop the handrail of a walkway that overlooked a beach, their doting young husbands standing next to them.

"Yes, we were in Cannes. We were both on our honeymoons." Jacqueline thought for a moment.

"That was when Jonas was stationed at Chambley-Bussières Air Base. See," May pointed at the photo, "he was in his uniform. Oh, he was so handsome." She smiled. "I remember asking my father to pay for an airline ticket, so we could be married. Oh," she remembered, "it was so expensive."

She sat quietly for a moment and then asked Jacqueline, "How have you managed since Maurice died? I know that I am lonely all of the time since Jonas passed."

"People tell you that it will get easier, and I suppose certain things do. However, although it has been over twenty years since Maurice passed, I have an emptiness that is there from the moment I wake up in the morning."

"I don't believe it will ever get easier for me." May took Jacqueline's hands in hers. "I'm grateful for our friendship, Jacqueline. It helps me remember. I so look forward to your letters and phone calls and your visits." May sat back then slid photo toward Jacqueline "Surely you'd like to keep this for yourself."

"No my dear, it is a gift. I want you to have it." She explained.

May sensed some hesitation from Jacqueline. "Jacqueline, are you alright? It seems like there is something on your mind."

"I need to tell you something and it is sad." She opened her purse and pulled out a handkerchief, "It's almost too sad to say out loud." She dabbed her eyes.

"Please tell me. Are you ill? We've been friends for fifty years. We've been through everything together. You can tell me anything Jacqueline."

"So I shall," Jacqueline took a deep breath. "I am sorry to say that travel has become too difficult for me and," she paused. "And, *this* will be my last trip, I am afraid." A tear dislodged itself from her eyelash and rolled down her cheek,

"I am afraid that we shall never see each other again." She could barely finish her sentence.

Seated side by side, they instinctively wrapped their arms tightly around one another. Their embrace was that of genuine love, devotion, and the pain of knowing that after fifty years, this would be their last meeting. The feeling of loss was staggering for them. Several minutes passed and they did not move, not wanting to let go.

The other hotel guests sensed the moment so profound, so personal, that they unconsciously averted their eyes to allow the ladies their privacy.

They both knew this day would come. How did time pass so quickly? It seemed like just yesterday they were on the beach in Santa Margarita, or playing tennis in La Jolla. Somewhere along the way concerns about age, stamina, health, and ability replaced spontaneity and light-hearted fun.

When the ladies released each other, they sat back in their chairs with tears in their eyes.

"I suppose we'll just have to rely on the telephone and our letters." Jacqueline tried to sound stoic.

May dabbed her eyes with a tissue and added with a forced smile. "To be truthful Jacqueline, I think I expected that one of us would die before we would have to experience this."

"Well then, my dear May, since we're not dead, let us make the most of our visit, shall we?" Jacqueline raised her glass in a toast. "À mon ami le plus cher et à nos souvenirs." Then she translated, "To my dearest friend and to our memories."

5:00 P.M.

Hank Mumser pushed through the hotel lobby revolving doors and checked his watch as if he timed his walking pace. He returned from his one-day, full-city solo-sightseeing extravaganza. Earlier in the day his wife, Mary Margaret, opted out of the day's activity. *Something about a leisurely day or some other foolishness*, Hank recalled. He tapped the face of his watch with his index finger. *Perfect*, he was pleased with himself. It was four fifty-eight, just in time for dinner. He and "the wife" always ate dinner at five o'clock on the dot. That way there was always enough time to eat, watch the news, and fully digest his meal before hitting the hay at nine or nine-thirty. Hank intended to be on the road early tomorrow morning for the six-hour drive and get home at a reasonable hour.

He went directly up to their hotel room to get Mary Margaret for dinner. She would no doubt be interested in what Hank did and saw during the day. Perhaps she had moved past the temper tantrum she threw earlier in the morning. *What kind of nonsense was that?* Hank thought. *A plan is a plan. And I had set the sightseeing plan ahead of time. The next thing you know, she gets in a mood and insists on a leisurely day. Oh, for heaven's sake.* He shrugged. *It must be that time of the month.*

As Hank walked toward the room, he decided that he would forgive her antics of the morning. After all, she had missed out. They would have a light dinner in the coffee shop downstairs and that would be that. When he opened the door, stepped into the room, and looked around, it was empty. Mary Margaret wasn't there. It was unusual for Mary Margaret not to be waiting for him and ready for dinner. It was, after all, five o'clock.

He went downstairs and looked in the gift shop, the dining room, and the pool area. Yet, on this day, Mary Margaret was nowhere to be found. Hank marched up to the desk clerk. "Oh, you're not the gal who was here this morning."

"No, sir, we had a shift change at two o'clock. I am Lillian Levine. May I be of assistance?" Lillian, the customer service liaison, was manning the desk while a coworker was taking a break.

"Yes, well. Have you seen my wife?" He seemed embarrassed and impatient.

"Well, sir, I'm not sure. What does she look like?" She smiled politely.

"You know," he said. "She's average." He held his hand about five feet off the ground. "She's about yea high, a little over five feet tall. Brownish or light brownish, greyish hair. She's fifty-two years old . . ."

Lillian laughed to herself; Hank had described every middle-aged woman at her gym, the supermarket, dry cleaners, on the bus . . . on earth. "I see." She remained polite. "What is she wearing?"

"Oh, I don't know. Who pays attention to that kind of thing? Her name is Mary Margaret Mumser. Have you seen her? Or did she leave a message for me?"

Lillian looked through a stack of guest messages. "No, sir, I don't think so. But if I see or hear from her, I will certainly let you know." She offered. "Did you check the bar?"

"No, she doesn't drink." Hank laughed at the notion. Hank only allowed beer at the house. He enjoyed a cold beer when he was watching "the game" or working in the garage. Mary Margaret, he thought, just enjoyed coffee, iced tea, or the occasional diet soda.

"Do you know where she is supposed to be?" Lillian asked. "Perhaps I can make a call for you?"

"All I know," Hank insisted, "is that she's supposed to be here. It's dinner time."

"Well, sir, maybe she's just running late. The traffic in the city can be quite heavy at this time of the day. Shall I call you in your room when she arrives? Or, would you like to sit in the lobby and wait for her?"

"I'll wait there." He pointed then marched over to the sofa where he planted himself, positioned to have a clear view of the revolving doors. When she returned, he was going to give her a piece of his mind. Going off on her own was one thing, but making him wait for dinner was something else altogether.

Although he watched the door like a sniper, for the next several hours, every hour on the hour he would walk over to the desk clerk to find out if he or she had seen Mary Margaret. "Could you please call the room and see if she is there?" Hank would ask, "She may have snuck past me and if she didn't, I don't want her to miss me when she comes in." This ritual continued throughout the evening and his irritation turned to worry.

It had been merely seconds since the clock struck five and the double doors of the large conference room seemed to explode outward. Out spilled pale, glassy-eyed business people all dressed in uncomfortable slate blue, grey, and black-colored business suits. At first, they wandered around like a goat rodeo, waiting for their eyes to adjust to the light after being held captive in a windowless room that was kept at meat locker temperatures for the past nine hours, enduring one Power Point presentation after another.

Into the lobby they spilled. Overly loud and peppy, they were trying to jolt their bodies and minds out of suspended animation. The women, no matter the size, in pencil skirts scurried in the general direction of the lobby ladies' rest-room. The sound of pantyhose material rubbing together was is deafening. Once inside, they wasted no time checking to see if the waist and thigh bands of their Spanx had finally cut through their skin or if this was the day that their internal organs were displaced by a foundation garment. "Does work-er's compensation cover this?" one woman asked another.

The rest of the crowd avalanched into the bar for the phase two of the day's conference activities. For the next hour they had to participate in mandatory schmoozing, forced friendship, and artificial familiarity before they headed to the another ballroom for phase three, a buffet dinner where they would carbo-load for phase four, the after-dinner and corporately-mandated dancing, drinking, and inappropriate behavior with coworkers.

Because this gathering was a business meeting, and serious highly-confidential and hard-hitting information such as the new policies about taking and distributing meeting notes and reserving conference rooms, the correct use of the lunch-room bulletin board, next year's holiday schedule, and the reminder of what is considered "Casual" for Casual Fridays, no spouses or witnesses were invited.

In the bar, blowhard executives and wannabes tossed their credit cards and room numbers at the bartender, offering to "pick this one up" for a person or group they wanted to impress or repress. A number of *the gals* stated that they "had to be careful" and started out ordering wine spritzers, knowing all too well that after a stiff one or two all bets would be off and the uptight, stayed, and controlled personas would be tossed aside as they busted a move on the dance floor and started telling people what they really thought of them. Married men who were rarely allowed a boys-night-out and were otherwise dork-ish suddenly felt handsome and virile as they told stories, falsifying—or at the very least enhancing—their personal histories. And why not? What happens at company meeting stays at a company meeting. Or does it?

There is always someone who is counting drinks. Serious damage can be done during pre-dinner cocktails. If all her peers are ordering wine spritzers, you can bet money that tongues will wag as Marla Krupnick orders a boiler maker. Conversely, if all men were ordering bourbon and Sean Phallus orders a cosmopolitan, the 'good-ol-boys' will have to be extra careful about telling him off-colored jokes or they would be forced to attend sensitivity training.

One by one, new and junior members of the company approached Joselyn Rydell, the president and co-founder of Master Flash to introduce themselves and hopefully make a lasting impression.

Instead of going straight to the bar with his coworkers, young Mr. Waters went back to his room to freshen up. He stripped off his suit and shirt, took a quick shower, applied cologne, combed his hair, brushed his teeth, and then he gargled. He chose a fresh, unwrinkled suit and shirt from the closet then redressed and reapplied his "Hello My Name Is" tag. He was ready for the evening's activities.

When Curtis Waters walked into the bar, he took a deep breath in then exhaled and walked up to the president of the company. "Ma'am? Excuse me, ma'am? Joselyn? Ms. Rydell? Joselyn?"

She knew she couldn't ignore the young man standing behind her forever. She turned her head and smiled. "Yes?" It was a deep and assertive yes, meant to be a frightening "yes." She was stunning. She had flawless skin and a lush mane of auburn hair. She was tall and slender but curvy at the same time.

He extended his hand, "We haven't had the chance to meet yet. Miss Rydell, I wanted to introduce myself. I'm Curtis, Curtis Waters. I'm the associate assistant to Tripp Matthews."

Although neither name rang a bell with her, she answered. "Oh yes, it's nice to meet you, uh?"

"Please call me Curt." He lowered his hand.

"Right, yes. Curt." She appreciated the save. "Tell me, Curt," she smiled then asked a cursory question. "How are you enjoying Master Flash life?"

He thought he would have to wait much longer, further into the conversation before he had an in, but there it was. "Truthfully, Miss Rydell, I'm underutilized." He stepped back slightly, smoothed his hair and unbuttoned his suit jacket and awaited her response.

He got her attention with his bold statement. She turned her whole body to squarely face him. "I see, Curt." She looked at him. She was humored by his nerve yet intrigued as well. "What position would you like to be in?"

"Oh, Ms. Rydell," He intentionally loosened his tie, as enticement. He leaned in and whispered, "I'm sure I would enjoy any position you would suggest." He winked then added, "I think we both would."

It took her a few seconds, but then she detected his play. "Well, Curt, you've got some balls. I'll tell you that."

He raised his eyebrows. "I'm not sure what you're referring to, but I wanted to come over and say hello, introduce myself and let you know that I am *eager* to please." He let his statement linger for a minute then continued. "Hey, this is a party, maybe not the best place for me to tell you what I can do to, ah... for you. However, if you have the time, I'd love to meet with you privately to find out what you—er, Master Flash needs and how I can give it to you." He took her hand in his. "It was a pleasure meeting you, Joselyn. I'll look forward to working more closely with you." Then Curt stepped away.

Joselyn stood there frozen for a minute. Had she just been propositioned by a new employee? Or had she been on the road so long, and focused for so long, that she misconstrued his conversation?

"There you are." Meredith Stringer, one of the company's vice presidents walked up. She saw the confused look on Joselyn's face and asked, "Are you alright?"

Without really moving she answered, "I think so. I just think I'm tired."

"Well, we're almost done. Come on, let's go. You have to make a speech when everyone comes in for dinner." She looked at her watch, "Which is about five minutes from now."

As they walked through the lobby toward the ballroom where dinner was to be served Joselyn asked, "Do we have a young male employee by the name of . . ." she stopped for a moment. "Isn't that funny, I've forgotten his name. It started with a K. Was it Kirk, or Ken, or something like that?"

"Oh," Meredith thought for a minute, "you know me, I can never remember anyone's name."

6:00 P.M.

Hand in hand and flush-faced from the excitement of the day, Nancy and Clark arrived back at the hotel. What a thrill it was to see San Francisco.

"And tomorrow," Clark offered as they walked into the lobby, "We'll see even more."

Phillpe noticed them as they walked in. He waved slightly in an effort to catch Clark's attention. When Clark looked at him, Phillipe offered him a strong-jawed and confident nod.

"Honey," Clark took Nancy over to the sofa. "Sit down for a minute and I'll be right back."

"Is there something wrong?"

"Oh no, nothing. I'm sure. I just need to go over there for a minute."

Phillipe met Clark half way and whispered in his French accent. "Sir, we are ready when you are."

Clark felt around in his pockets making sure that the ring box was where he had expected it to be. He was excited and looked like a little boy as he straightened his hair and jacket. "How do I look?"

"Fine, sir. Please have a seat next to your wife and we will be ready to begin in a minute."

"What's going on?" Nancy was confused and asked Clark as he sat down next to her.

He patted her hands. "Nothin'. I don't know, really. You know how I am. I'm not used to everything so fancy."

A waiter arrived with a tray and on it a bottle of champagne, glasses, and a candle. He placed it in front of them on the low lobby table. "Compliments of the Shipley Hotel's management, Monsieur et Madame March." As if timed perfectly, as soon as the cork was popped, the lobby's string quartet started playing.

Clark fished around in his pocket. Nancy was very uncomfortable, her cheeks turned red. Embarrassed, she looked to Clark for comfort.

"Don't worry, honey. *This* is for you." He motioned at the champagne and violinist. "You deserve it. You have put up with my sorry butt for so long. Sometimes . . . no, *most* of the time I don't think I deserve you. You are such a good mother. You made sure that our kids were good and smart. They're smarter than me by far. You made sure we were all taken care of, that they went to school and then even graduated from college. I don't know how you did it. But they are good people with futures. I'm so proud." He wiped his tears with the back of his hand.

"*We* did it, Clark. You worked as hard as I did." She raised her glass. "Here's to us, Clark."

Clark spilled a little champagne on his windbreaker. "Damn." He looked across the room at the concierge, who was on the phone and winked at Clark.

"What's the matter, Clark?" Nancy dabbed his coat with a napkin. "You seem so nervous."

"Oh hell, Nan, I am." He cleared his throat. "I was wondering. It is our thirtieth anniversary, and I was wondering if you would still marry me all these years later if I were to propose today."

"Now you're being silly." She smiled.

He reached into his pocket and pulled out the ring box. "Nancy, my love." He kneeled in front of her. "I know this is thirty years late, but . . ." he opened the box then looked into Nancy's eyes. "This is an engagement ring, the one I couldn't afford back then. I want you to have it now."

Nancy's eyes welled up with tears. It took merely seconds before they spilled down her cheeks. She grabbed a cocktail napkin to dab her face. "Oh, Clark, you didn't have to . . ."

"Yes, I did." He sat next to her again. "I have always loved you. So I'm askin', if you had it to do all over again, would you still marry me?"

Nancy blushed like she did when he originally asked her when she was seventeen years old. "I would marry you all over again. Yes." She kissed him.

The concierge approached with a tray of petit fours and signaled to the waiter to step up and refresh their glasses of champagne. "May I get your folks anything el—" Phillipe feigned surprise, placed his hand over his heart, and asked the beaming Nancy, "Is that an engagement ring?"

That was the queue. Joe, Beth, Amy, and Meg came rushing from their hiding place near the bar. They were all dressed for a formal wedding. Joe was in a tuxedo and the girls were wearing dresses in different shades of pink.

Months earlier, when Meg told her siblings of Clark's plans to propose again, they concocted a plan and all made arrangements to be there. Arriving in San Francisco from their homes in Arkansas, South Carolina New Mexico, and Arizona, they had been sneaking around to be certain that Clark and Nancy didn't catch a glimpse of them and blow their surprise.

It worked! Both Clark and Nancy were incredibly surprised. "What?" Nancy cried.

"What are you doing here?" Clark asked, through his tears.

"Well, we couldn't let you get married without us," Meg beamed.

"We're the bridesmaids," Amy added.

"Married again?" Clark didn't know what was going on. "What do you mean . . . ?"

Just then the concierge motioned for the string quartet to move closer and begin setting up chairs and music stands.

Hal, the florist, walked through the lobby, delivering a cart filled with floral bouquets and boutonnieres for the occasion. His next stop was at the boutique to gather Pamela for their date. He hoped that she would be willing to join him. He stopped for a moment to look at his reflection in a lobby mirror. Benny had helped him pick out the perfect "first date" clothes: freshly-pressed grey slacks, a starched white shirt opened at the collar, and a pair on loafers. "Rugged and masculine, with a touch of panache," Benny said as he snapped his fingers. "I'd go out with you." As he was headed out the door, Benny reminded him, "You have dinner reservations at Blanca's at seven. It's on the wharf. I've asked for a table by the window." He put a folded piece of paper in his hand. "Fernando is the maître d'. He's my . . . ah . . . friend. Just let him know if you need anything." Ben walked his father to the front door and pushed him through. "Now go," he said, pretending to be a mother sending her child off to school for the first time, "before I begin to cry."

Just as Hal got to the lobby boutique he saw Pamela locking the sliding gate. His heart sunk. But when she stood up and turned around, she had a huge grin on her face. "Hal? I'll be ready to go in a minute. I need to deliver this veil to the bride in the lobby."

"Great," Hal smiled with relief. "I'll go with you."

The quartet was playing Pachelbel's Canon in D. The hotel guests in and around the lobby area began gathering, wondering what was going on.

Phillipe walked to the center of the lobby. "Pardon me, Sirs and Madams, may I have your attention, s'il vous plaît? You are all invited to attend the impromptu wedding of Monsieur and Madame March. They have been *mari et femme* for thirty years, and these fine ladies and gentleman," he pointed to Meg, Joe, Amy, and Beth, "are their four children who have arranged this ceremony for them. I would like to ask you all to take out your cameras and mobile phones and be so kind as to record this occasion for them. I would like to provide you with an email address where you may send these pictures so they will have a remembrance of the day and perhaps for you to keep to remind you of what true love is."

After hearing the announcement Jacqueline turned toward her friend May and offered, "You see May, romance is still alive." The two little ladies stood up, and then arm-in-arm they walked across the lobby to attend the event.

Hank Mumser turned to watch from his post where he had been sitting, waiting for Mary Margaret to return. Oscar Pasternak repositioned his chair so he could watch too.

From the pool area and wrapped in damp towels, Darlene and Brad were walking through the lobby toward the elevators and noticed people gathering. "Now what?" Darlene seemed exasperated.

Brad looked around. There were flowers and what appeared to be bridesmaids, a man in a tuxedo, and a woman in a veil, and he heard a string quartet playing. He smiled. "I think there's going to be a wedding, honey."

"What?" she made a sour face. "In the lobby?" She exhaled, "I don't understand why people have to make a spectacle out of everything. We got married in a church. We had a reception and ate some cake and that was that. No fireworks, no marching band, no nothing and see, we're still married." She looked at the kids, "Let's go." She pointed at the elevator bank. "Now go push the button and we'll be right there."

"Sure we are—still married, I mean." He motioned towards the group preparing for the ceremony, "But . . ."

"But what, Brad?" she huffed, "What about romance? What about love? What are you going to do? We have the kids and responsibilities. If you made more money, maybe we would have the luxury . . ." She looked at the defeated expression on Brad's face. "I still have love for you, but things have changed."

Natalie Guilfoyle and Patrick Montgomery had just returned to the hotel from their adventure-with-a-stranger day. Natalie couldn't remember having such a perfect and surprising day. The thought of work never entered her mind. She never imagined that simply walking through a city could be so magical. The pace and the conversation had been easy, and for the first time in years, she was completely relaxed and comfortable with a man, with a stranger, on a date. She even ate a hamburger . . . with a bun! *And* French fries! Carbohydrates be damned, by noon she was love-struck.

They took a moment and watched the activity at the far end of the lobby. Natalie turned to Patrick and asked, "I know I said I wanted to go upstairs and change my clothes for dinner, but do you mind if we stand here for a minute?"

"No, not at all, Nat," Patrick smiled. He took her hand in his. He was smitten. "This seems perfect."

As hotel staff members and conference goers spilled into the lobby, cellphone cameras were readied and a young man in a formal-dress army uniform walked over to the couple with a bible in his hand.

"Are you a real priest?" Clark was wide-eyed. All of this was such a surprise.

"Sir, I am Army Chaplain Douglas Canton stationed at Fort Bragg, and it is my honor to marry you and your lovely wife today. Sir," he stepped back, "please take your bride's hand."

Chaplain Canton began by thanking the family for allowing others to witness this beautiful event. He discussed the values of marriage and then shared the story of how Clark and Nancy met, married, and raised a family. Meg beamed. She had provided this information to Phillipe who clearly had provided it to the chaplain, who was so eloquent. When the chaplain asked the couple to say a few words in the form of impromptu wedding vows, he couldn't help but notice that they seemed uncomfortable in front of a crowd of strangers, so he instructed Meg, Joe, Beth, and Amy to link arms and form a semicircle, a shield of sorts around their parents, creating an intimate space for them. Within this space, they said their vows.

"Clark," Nancy started with tears in her eyes, "if anyone asked me yesterday, I would have said that I was the luckiest girl in the world and that you were the sweetest man anyone could ever wish for. And today . . ." she bit her lip and tried to collect herself. She looked at their children then whispered, "Thank you."

The chaplain wiped the tears from his eyes. "Mr. March, sir, do you have a few words for Nancy?"

"Oh, Nan, you know how I feel about you . . ." He inhaled with a stutter, trying so hard to keep from crying, and he looked at the chaplain for assistance.

"Thank you, sir. There is no doubt about how you two feel." He gave them a moment then asked the children to break their circle, allowing the crowd to celebrate with them.

Chaplain Canton cleared his throat and began. "Do you, Nancy, take Clark . . ."

Out of character, Nancy interrupted the chaplain, "I do."

"Okay," Douglas Canton couldn't help but smile. "Now Clark, do you take Nancy to be . . ."

"I do, and I did, and I would again a hundred times over." He smiled.

"Well then, it is my honor—no," he corrected himself, "it is a true privilege for me to pronounce you husband and wife again. You may kiss your bride."

As Clark tenderly kissed his bride, the quartet began to play, the crowd applauded, people searched for tissues to wipe their tears, and the chef appeared, rolling out a cart holding a multi-tiered wedding cake for everyone to enjoy.

Nancy and Clark were overwhelmed. Just out of high school they rushed off to the courthouse. There wasn't any music or fresh flowers or cake, just their desire to begin their life together. Before they knew it thirty years had passed, and they had grown children.

When Clark tasted the wedding cake, he turned to the chef and said, "Thank you. Your cake is good, but it's not as good as Nancy's."

"Excuse me, sir," a quiet voice asked from across the desk. Charlie turned around. It was Jenny, the new bellman. Charlie's stomach jumped a little.

"Yes, hi. I'm Charlie," he said softly, almost as if he was afraid that his full voice would knock her over. "Is there something I can do for you . . . ?"

"Jenny," she blushed. "I'm Jenny from . . ." she pointed toward the bell desk. "I was wondering if you could help me, please." She pointed over to where Oscar was sitting. "I think there's a problem?" She looked frightened and she put her hands over her mouth. A second later she cupped her hands around her lips and mouthed, "I think he's dead."

Charlie leaned over the desk and looked over at Oscar. He was slumped sideways in his chair, his mouth open and his eyes closed. "Oh, that's Mr. Pasternak. Sometimes he falls asleep." Charlie tried to assure Jenny, "There's nothing to worry about."

"Are you sure? Because he doesn't seem to be breathing, and when I tried to check his wrist for a pulse . . ." she shrugged, "nothing."

Charlie turned to Connie and Vicky and all the color had left his face. "I think Mr. Pasternak is dead. What should we do?"

Vicky picked up the phone receiver, "I'll call the paramedics, and Connie, you call security. Charlie," she looked over to the area where Mr. Pasternak's body was, "you go sit over there and make sure no one gets near him. Act like you're talking to him or something."

Charlie pulled a chair over and sat next to Mr. Pasternak and proceeded to silently move his lips and make animated gestures, thinking that if anyone looked over at them it would appear as if he and Oscar were involved in conversation.

After about a minute or two Charlie heard, "What the hell are you doing? You look like a nut." Oscar sat up straight. "Can't a guy take a nap?"

Charlie looked over at the front desk. Vicky and Connie were laughing and high-fiving each other. Through her laughter Connie said, "Gotcha, rookie. Welcome to the Shipley!"

7:00 P.M.

Alisa and Tom's affair began the day they met four years earlier at a neighborhood block party. While their families enjoyed a bouncy house and mayonnaise-soaked coleslaw, their trip to get more soft drinks turned into them fucking in a neighbor's garage.

They understood each other. Living in suburbia was like a life sentence for both of them. Their affair was about two things: the sex and getting away with it. Their spouses seemed to be oblivious about their relationship, and that excited them even more. It was a game. Most of the time, Alisa and Tom pretended like they hardly noticed one another, then once every few weeks they'd slip away to a predetermined locale for a rendezvous.

Alisa had been a Las Vegas showgirl when she met and married her husband Michael, a recently divorced single dad. Although at the time she thought settling down with a family was what she wanted, she quickly realized she had gotten herself trapped in a life of PTA, carpooling, and barbecues with women wearing culottes and Easy Spirits. It didn't even come close to fulfilling her. Michael had promised her exotic trips and excitement, but his career as a motivational speaker always came first. So, she found other things and other men to provide the excitement she wasn't getting at home.

It wasn't that Tom was dissatisfied with his marriage and life with his wife Karen; he simply couldn't keep his dick in his pants. He guessed that he had some personal or personality flaw, but he didn't care enough to do anything about it. He loved the risk and excitement. Since Karen said she had forgiven him when she caught him having a fling years earlier, whether she knew it or not, she had unwittingly resigned herself to life with a philanderer. Her forgiveness was her own undoing.

"I called ahead. I'll go get the room key. Why don't you take your sexy little body to the bar and order us a couple of drinks." Tom patted Alisa on the ass when they entered the lobby. "We'll have a drink and then head up to the room."

"Hey, handsome," Alisa called to the bartender as she sat down on a stool at the bar. "How about two of your special vodka martinis? You know how I like 'em. Just pass the vermouth bottle over the glasses." Maxim winked at her and nodded. She was a familiar face at the lobby bar.

"Hi, Max." Tom greeted Maxim as he sat down.

"Sir, it's good to see you and your lovely lady again. If you're not good to her, I might steal her away." Although it was just polite barman banter, Alisa ate it up.

"You heard him?" She slapped Tom's arm playfully.

"What would Michael say if you snuck off with Maxim?" Tom played along.

"Oh, you know Michael. He'd rationalize it and say something about my need for attention." She laughed. "You don't need a PhD for that."

"Hey, a lot of people pay to hear him speak about living life and being in touch with emotions." Tom sipped his drink then sat quietly for a minute. There was something on his mind. "Alisa, I was wondering. Do you think they know? I mean about us. Do you think Michael has any idea?"

"Oh come on." Alisa dismissed the thought. "I don't think he has a clue about anything. I doubt he would care. His only concern is that I take care of his kids. His ex-wife is nowhere to be found and I'm the babysitter. Anyway, he's always on a business trip or at some client dinner, anyway. That's where he is tonight. I even suggested that he stay overnight in town. So, when you texted me, I dropped off the kids at his mother's house for a sleepover and told her I needed a night to myself. She was thrilled." Alisa laughed, "So it's a win–win for everyone." She put her hand between Tom's legs.

"What?" He instinctually moved her hand. "Michael's here? In town?" Tom knew having an affair with his friend's wife was one thing, but being caught was quite another.

"Yes, but don't worry. He'd never stay here. He always stays at some motel near the Marina District. Relax. It's nothing to wet your pants over."

"Karen doesn't have any idea either." He calmed himself. "She's so busy with the kids. They're her main focus, anyway. Even though she said she did, I know that she never really forgave me when I had that affair a million years ago. I apologized but I don't think it made a difference. We're just going through the motions at this point. She even sent the kids on an overnight at the neighbors because she doesn't trust that I'd pay enough attention to them while she's away for the evening."

Alisa joked, "She's out for the evening? Aren't you afraid she's having an affair?"

"No—are you kidding? Not Karen." He laughed at the idea. "She's spending the evening with her friend Winnie. I don't care much for her, and she absolutely hates me. She takes every opportunity to badmouth me. For years she was trying to get Karen to leave me or have an affair to even the score."

"I won't badmouth you," she kissed his neck and cooed into his ear, "unless you want me to." For the next several minutes they nuzzled, kissed deeply, and caressed each other, making people around them uncomfortable. The truth was that they really had very little to talk about, so their conversation was usually short-lived. The relationship was about sex, not exchanging ideas.

But on this night, Tom was chatty. "What would you do if Michael found out about us?"

"I doubt he'd do anything except talk it to death, dissecting it down to its simplest elements until it had no meaning." She laughed and added sarcastically, "I think the worst thing that would happen is that the summer barbecues would be awkward for a while. Oh hell, Tommy, Michael actually thinks you're his best friend, that's how stupid he is."

Tom set down his drink on the bar. "Boy, Alisa, that's a cruel thing to say."

"Oh come on, Tom, we're not here because we're nice people." She finished her drink and flagged down the bartender for another.

Tom knew that he was a self-serving and dishonest husband but, until that moment, he had never considered himself cruel. He thought about it for a few minutes. He knew that he treated his home and Karen and the kids like an obligation, but he had always prided himself in being a good provider, and he spent weekends and holidays with them. Maybe he wasn't as nice as he thought he was.

Alisa could see that he was deep in thought. If they were going to have a fun and wild night, he needed to snap out of it. "Oh lighten up, Tommy. It's not as if we're going to run off together and buy a minivan or an above-ground pool. We're just fucking. Just order another drink and relax."

8:00 P.M.

At the far end of the lobby a crowd was gathering for a thirtieth high school reunion. A huge maroon and silver colored banner that read "Welcome Class of 1985 Titans!" was hung over a long table covered with a correspondingly colored tablecloth. On it were neatly organized rows of "Hello My Name Is" name tags.

Women in bedazzled gowns with unflattering deep-diving cleavage cuts and men in slacks and sports jackets milled around the sign-in and name badge table. Polite nods and "how ya been doin'" passed for greetings. The lies were flying, "You look fabulous, younger than ever." "You are more beautiful (or handsome) than I remember." "I meant to keep in touch." "Let's exchange numbers before we leave." iPhone cameras were flashing furiously as dozens of people simultaneously sucked in their guts, and extended their necks to give the illusion that they had only one chin and, as far as anyone in the room would admit, none of them had changed "a bit" in thirty years.

The sign-in table volunteers were managed by the caf-feine-charged Becky Thorton who headed the reunion committee. Becky's excitement was at a fever pitch. This event was the highlight of her life. Through a constant barrage of annoying emails and Facebook and LinkedIn invitations, she managed to stalk or keep track of most of her senior class-mates. She spent years compiling, sorting, and resorting the list until . . . Ooh! It was time to send out the invitations for the reunion. For the six months leading up to the reunion date, she would recite her activities to anyone who stood still long enough to listen. "I designed and printed the invitations, planned the reunion, managed the responses, booked the venue, booked the band, booked a bank of rooms, arranged for valet parking, determined the menu, created the seating chart," and worked herself up into such a whirling tizzy that her husband was planning on booking her into rehab.

Stepping up to the table, a stout woman announced, "I'm Suzie Uker, uh . . ." she corrected herself, "My maiden name was Cox. Look for Suzanne Cox." She craned her neck trying to find her name tag. "There it is, Suzanne Cox-Uker."

Former Prom Queen, pep club captain, expert blow-jobber, and occasional church-goer Suzie Uker was now 260 pounds of Avon pusher. Her perfectly made-up face with Cleopatra eyeliner was topped with a pile of yellow cake-colored curls. The former Miss Cox was now living "in the valley" with her husband Mark, the former class quarterback who was now a 350-pound man who looked like a pile of kielbasa. Mark often wore tank tops, thinking he was passing off his gelatinous rolls as muscle when he said "Yup, I played ball in high school" while he patted his rotund physique. Early on, both too popular to be concerned about grades or their futures, Suzie never applied for college and Mark lost his sports-scholarship. He worked for his father's insurance company franchise and they had three children who had rotten teeth and diabetes. Suzie pressed Mark's name tag onto his ill-fitting sports coat and told him to find the bar while she looked for old friends. She spotted and waved at a group of gals in coordinaed outfits. She desperately hoped they'd recognize her.

The four former cheerleaders who had remained friends for the three decades since graduation clearly coordinated their outfits for the occasion, and they were all wearing similar sleeveless shift dresses, upper-arm flab be damned.

"Ready, and!" The forty-somethings with midriff bulk enthusiastically executed their old cheerleader moves as they greeted each other. "Aaaaaaaaand go Titans!" Their cheer was accompanied by happy, tiny bent elbow handclaps. Thrilled that they attracted the attention in the room, they popped up and down on their toes and executed above-the-head air punches accompanied with "woo-hoos" to stir up the crowd.

"Oh, I miss those days," said Claire, a frequent recipient of plastic surgery services. "You have to admit we still look good."

Head cheerleader Patricia Conrad-Blake spotted a stunning woman who walked toward the sign-in table. "Who's that?" she said with a catty tone.

Claudia Schulman, formerly a regularly overlooked bookworm in corrective shoes was now a stunner in a smart-looking, perfectly fitted red dress. With a roller-bag behind her and while wrapping up a business call on her cellphone, she walked up to the sign-in and name tag table. "Claudia Schulman," she said to the volunteer high school senior who was manning the name tag desk.

"Did I hear you say Claudia Schulman?" A handsome man wearing a dark suit inquired.

Claudia turned around and said her goodbyes to the person on the other end of her phone call. "Yes, I'm Claudia Schulman." It took her a minute but she did recognize the man standing in front of her. "Matthew Gold." She smiled widely. "It's so nice to see you."

"You look wonderful, Claudia." He glanced at her travel bag on wheels. "I take it you don't live here anymore."

"No, I live in New York now and I had to be in town for a business meeting next week and figured, why not come to the reunion." She flagged down a bellman and asked him to store her bag until she checked in. "Matthew, what are you up to? The last thing I remember is that you were headed to Stanford and you were going to be a great inventor of futuristic devices."

"I can't believe you remembered." He was flattered. Being a "nerd" in high school, he never thought anyone paid attention to him. "Right. Yes, I went to Stanford and eventually entered a master's program to begin working on the development of alternative and electric transportation."

"Like the hybrid and electric cars?"

"Yes, but more recently, high speed rail transportation." Though happy to see Claudia, he had dreaded the idea of attending the reunion but his wife, Sharon, insisted that he come, saying that he deserved a night of I-told-you-so. "Tell me, Claudia, what are you doing now, in New York no less?"

"Oh," she was humble, "I'm in international law."

"How wonderful. It's a far cry from when they used to call us 'Nerdella' and 'Geekman.'"

Claudia laughed. "But I was a nerd and a geek. And, that was a million years ago."

Rachel Mallinger walked up to Claudia, "Claud. I'm glad you could make it. Otherwise, I'd have a quick drink and get out of here."

"Matthew, do you remember Rachel Mallinger, another member of the high school geek society?" She turned to her longtime friend Rachel, "Rach, do you remember Matthew Gold?"

"Oh yes," Matthew reached out to shake Rachel's hand. "And, one of my companies contracted with Rachel to do a reorganization of the workforce. What was it? Six years ago?"

"Hi, Matt. It's great to see you." She grasped his hand in hers. "How's Sharon? Is she here?"

"She's here, somewhere." he looked around. "She's probably punishing someone for being cruel to me thirty years ago." His eyes twinkled as he talked about his wife. "It's great to be married to the president of my fan club."

"Let's find Sharon and go get a cocktail. I think we'll need one or two to make it through this evening."

Greg Thomas, former average student with an eye for the girls, especially those who had zero interest in him, pointed across the room and asked the small group who he was standing with, "Isn't that the Ti-Per-Pow business celebrity, Rachel Mallinger? You know, she's that author and in all of those magazines."

"Oh yeah, that's her," said Beatrice "Bea" Holmes, née Barker, the former broad-shouldered captain of the girls swim and softball teams, now a manly-looking woman and married to scrawny, mealy-mouthed Norbert Holmes. She had a short, gray, easy-to-care-for haircut and was wearing formal attire appropriate for a campout. She sneered, "I hear she's a lesbian."

"Weren't you friends with Rachel back then?" Greg raised his eyebrow.

"Yeah, well . . ." Not wanting to reveal her not-so-secret secret unrequited crush on Rachel, Bea redirected her attention, "Well would you look at what the cat dragged in, Joanne Flugal. She looks rough."

Joanne   Flugal-Ferrar-Cortez-Manning-Linderhausen, decked out in her sparkly, sequined evening gown, with the deep-V that was displaying what were now two opposite facing diagonal creases from which hung her sagging bosoms. She barked to her fourth husband, "Claus, get me a gin martini." With her cotton candy, over-processed hair, weatherworn, tanned leather skin, and lipstick creeping up the lines above her upper lip, she reeked of cigarettes. She struck a pose and began taking in the sights of the crowd, desperately hoping that someone would recognize her, even though she looked twenty years older than the rest of the women in the room. As a bit of an unpredictable nutcase, Joanne had few, if any, girlfriends in high school as she would insinuate herself into conversations and overwhelm them with nonsensical chatter.

Some people collect stamps; Joanne collected husbands. Using her body, bed skills, and repressed gag reflexes she easily attracted three far-sighted geezers to marry and sponsor her while she lived the high life. Once she hit her forties, sun and alcohol caught up and her appeal had faded, making it difficult to market herself even to the octogenarian set. Newer, fresher models were now available. Faced with having to support herself, she settled for and married Claus Linderhausen, a hardworking, younger man who needed a green card to stay in the country.

Joanne squinted at the name tags on people as they walked by. "Mary! Mary Warren!" She spotted someone familiar. "It's me, Joanne. Joanne Flugal." They had been friends for a short time during their senior year but had a falling out when Mary started dating someone that Joanne fancied.

Mary stopped and turned towards Joanne, whom she did not recognize.

"Mary, it's me, Joanne Flugal. Remember? We used to hang out and go to the football games together on Friday nights."

Nope, not ringing any bells; Mary had no idea who the woman standing in front of her was. "Oh, Joanne, of course I remember. How are you?" she politely lied.

"Great!" She grabbed Mary and hugged her tight. "You, my friend, look great!" Joanne continued. "Are you married? Do you have any kids? Where do you live now? You should give me your phone number. I know this great place for lunch . . ."

Joanne was just too animated. It made Mary uncomfortable. The rapid fire questions seemed desperate, but Mary remained gracious. "Yes. I've been married for eighteen years, we have three wonderful sons. How about you?" She deftly avoided the question about her location and the whole phone number request.

Joanne had been waiting for this moment. "Oh Mary, you know me, I was never one who liked to be alone. So, yes silly, I'm married." She playfully rolled her eyes. "He's number four." She added, "This one is the keeper. You know what they say. You have to kiss a lot of frogs . . ." Too excited to stop, she continued. "No, I never had children. Remember I used to have all those problems with my period? I'm sure you do. Well it turns out that I had endometriosis and some scaring on my ovaries, so I had a hysterectomy. Oh, what a nightmare that was. I ended up going into menopause in my early thirties. Oh God, my skin was dry, I had hot flashes, hair was appearing in places . . . and don't get me started about vaginal dryness."

Mary was horrified. She hated that she got herself roped into the conversation, but what could she do? Could she point across the room, and when Joanne turned to look, make a quick getaway? No—instead she tried to wrap up the conversation. "It was great seeing you . . ." Mary forgot her name, " . . . dear. But I was just on my way, uh, my husband is waiting."

Brad Wilkerson and Keith Wallace were inseparable in high school. They double dated together and exaggerated their sexual conquests to each other. They tried to remain friends over the years, but interests, opinions, and goals changed, coupled with the reality that high school popularity fades and the benefits or fallout from choices start to surface.

Secretly, they were each embarrassed by the choices that had made their lives miserable. Yet, Keith was convinced that Brad resented him for being more successful and having more money even though he had been in and out of jail a couple of times. Brad told himself that he and Keith drifted apart because their wives hated each other, and Brad had always been afraid to take risks. Both of them were right, but the overriding fact was that high school friendships don't always last forever.

Now, both at the reunion, having not seen or spoken to each other in more than ten years, they stood twenty feet apart and both posed as if they were going to draw their pistols—a stance they had taken on a daily basis back in high school.

"If you're not out of town by the time I count to three . . ." Brad hollered loudly to garner attention.

"Draw!" Keith shouted. And they both shot each other using their index-finger pistols.

"Buddy! How the hell have you been?" Keith stepped up to Brad and slapped him on the back.

"No effin' way, come here!" Brad grabbed and hugged Keith.

Keith stood next to Brad, taking in the sights. "Can you believe the fillies here? Women in their forties . . . easy pickin'." He chuckled. It was that certain kind of chuckle only made by jackasses and letches.

Brad looked around. "Hey, where's that wife of yours? I'm sure she wouldn't like to hear you talk that way."

Keith laughed, "Oh hell, she didn't like to hear a lot of things I had to say. She took the kids and left years ago. Hey, where's Darlene? Are you still together?"

"Oh yeah. She keeps me in line. Or at least that's what she thinks." Brad winked, trying to imply that he was some sort of a player. But it couldn't be further from the truth. Over the years Brad had turned into a full-blown nebbish who asked permission to do almost everything. Darlene didn't allow him to manage their money, think for himself or wear shoes in the house. He was on a schedule. Sunday morning he mowed lawn. Monday through Friday he was expected to be home by six o'clock and ready to sit down to dinner then wash dishes. Thursday night he took out the trashcans. Life couldn't be more mundane. For fun on a Saturday afternoon, he would sit on a chair in the bra department holding his wife's purse while she tried on underwear at Macy's. That or equally henpecked activities were usually followed by a light dinner and then home to watch Jeopardy. Sex was designated for holidays and birthdays—but only with the lights off.

"Come on, Brad." Darlene barked as she walked toward her husband with her hand out to collect him by his upper arm. "They're about ready to let everyone in, and I have no intention of waiting in a buffet line until the food is cold and picked over."

Embarrassed, Brad turned to Keith. "Sorry man. I'll see you inside." Then he turned and followed his wife toward the open double doors.

"'Thunder Stick,' is that you?" The voice came from behind them. "Yo man, Brad 'Thunder Stick' Wilkerson? I know that's you."

Brad turned around to see the one and only Lance Shall-we-dance, In-your-pants Cochran. All decked out in his high-waisted, sans-a-belt gabardine slacks so tight that you could see the detail of his fishnet underwear. Brad expected no less from him. "Hey, Pants Dancer, how's it hanging?"

"Mostly to the left." Lance made a hang-loose gesture with his hands and nodded his head like a bobble-head doll. "It's all cool. Hey," he looked over at the angry-looking, portly woman who was standing next to Brad. "Hey Thunder, is this your kitten?"

"Oh, yeah." He had forgotten she was still there. "Lance, this is my wife Darlene."

Lance figured that she either had to have looked better when Brad married her, or she was one of those freaky, ugly girls who was willing to do anything. "Hey babydoll," he winked at Darlene as he took Brad in a partial chokehold, "you must have to fight him off with a kitchen broom. In high school, this dog here was in more pants than a Calvin Klein label. Are you pickin' up what I'm puttin' down?" He looked over at Brad, "Do you still have that enormous schlong? Oh baby," he nudged Darlene with his elbow, "he shoulda hung a sign from it that said 'Caution: objects may appear closer than they actually are.' Man," he laughed, "Thunder, you should have handed out safety goggles . . ."

"Hey, Lance" Brad added. "Do you remember when you intentionally super glued your hands to Patricia Glassman's breasts?"

"Oh yeah," Lance was surprised that Brad came up with that one. "She lost some skin. I felt bad about that."

Darlene was disgusted. "I'm going in to find a seat. Are you coming?" Her tone could make skin chap.

As she stomped away, Lance called after her. "Don't be like that, babydoll. You'll see. I'm like olives. At first I seem salty and slimy, and you might not like me, but after a martini or two, you won't be able to get enough of me."

Brad had an enormous smile on his face and turned toward Lance. "Thanks man, you have no idea how much I enjoyed that. You *are* going to sit with us at our table, aren't you? I'm beggin' you."

"Everyone, everyone." Becky Thorton stood on a chair and waved her arms. "Can I have your attention, please? We will be moving our reunion into the Tapestry Ballroom. Find your tables, and grab your plate because . . ." She paused to build up the excitement. "it's a buffet! Get ready for some fun. At ten o'clock we have a slideshow and awards ceremony. Plus, I managed to book the band, The Fogies. So strap on your dancing shoes. I expect everyone to be boogying on the dance floor. Woo hoo!"

9:00 P.M.

Neither one of them planned to have an affair. Michael Zimmerman was Karen Compton's husband Tom's best friend. And although Karen wasn't close to Michael's wife Alisa, they socialized, sharing dinners out, parties, and play-dates with the kids. Michael, a motivational speaker, was known for being rational and charismatic. After all, it was his job. His spirited personality was usually passed off as engaging, playful repartee but his flirting wasn't innocent when it came to Karen, and she knew it. Despite being married to Tom, she felt a very strong attraction to Michael. It made her feel desirable, and as much as she wanted to deny it, it excited her.

She couldn't be one hundred percent sure, but Karen had a sneaking suspicion that her husband Tom had had several affairs during their marriage. She knew of one. It occurred several years earlier. It was with Tom's coworker, Ursula. She was exotic and sexy and available. When Karen confronted him, Tom confessed. He said he would end it and even changed his job. She knew he probably found another Ursula at his new place of work or at the gym, the gas station, or an ATM machine. Although she said she forgave him, Karen never completely trusted him after that. He knew it but he ignored it.

Over the years, Michael and Karen's attraction had grown more intense. Innocent flirting turned into stolen glances at barbecues and holiday parties. Simple kisses on the cheek and hugs hello and good-bye grew to mean more than what they were. Michael had to fight erections at summer swim parties. Karen explained away her red cheeks as being overheated or tired. Finally, during a summertime yard party, they found themselves alone in Karen's kitchen. Karen had made a decision. She was no longer going to fight his advances.

Standing at the kitchen sink, rinsing dishes, Karen gazed through the window to see her husband Tom rubbing suntan oil on Alisa's neck and shoulders—areas of her skin that she could have easily reached on her own. Besides, the oil was in one of those special ozone-free aerosol cans with the dual purpose of even coverage and *not* having to rub it in. *I knew it.* Karen shook her head. It couldn't have been more obvious if Alisa was giving Tom a blowjob on the patio.

Michael walked into the kitchen, "The kids need more ju—" Karen turned away from the window and toward him. She took a deep breath and looked at him in a way that she hadn't before. Michael stopped for a minute then quietly and carefully stepped toward her. The sexual tension was palpable. As they attempted to make strained small talk about the barbecued chicken, the weather, the kids, and the bouncy house something changed. Michael reached over, took Karen's hand in his, and whispered, "I'm not sure I can take this much more. I want—no, I need—to explore my feelings for you." Karen knew exactly what he was saying.

Karen swallowed. "I know," she said and squeezed his hand.

When Michael whispered, "I think we owe it to ourselves to find out what *this* is. Do you agree with me?"

She looked out the window again and said, "Yes, I do."

At nine o'clock the hotel's revolving doors spun and deposited Karen and Michael into the lobby. Michael had his hand on the small of her back as he led her toward the lobby sitting area. She was carrying a plastic bag. In it were the leftovers from dinner.

"Karen," he whispered as he set down the unfinished bottle of wine from the restaurant. "I'll go and see if they have a room."

"I know we don't have a reservation," he said to Lillian who was manning the front desk. "But I was hoping that you have one room available." He looked over at Karen.

"How many nights will you be staying with us, sir?" Lillian smiled.

"Ah, just one night, please." He blushed a little.

Lillian could see how uncomfortable Michael was. She could spot an affair from a hundred feet away. Married couples would approach the desk together. With those who were having an affair, only one of them would check-in while the other hung back, usually looking lost or guilty. "Ah yes, we do have a room available. It's on the fifteenth floor, and the view is lovely."

Michael was hardly listening. He was watching Karen. She was beautiful. She hadn't changed since he met her years earlier. He had to admit that his wife, Alisa, was beautiful too. She was smart and feisty, and she was a good step-mother to his kids. She also worked very hard to look her best, and he enjoyed knowing that other men found her attractive too. But there was just something about Karen, something deeper.

I must be crazy. Karen looked at the doggy bag. *What kind of a woman brings leftovers to an affair? What's the matter with me?* She had to laugh at herself. *Habit, I guess.* Tom loved leftovers, it was just his thing. Maybe it was because he was a cheap, who knew? If he could, he would never leave a restaurant without a doggy bag, even if it was filled with only a few free rolls. But it was his thriftiness that afforded them yearly vacations, late model cars, and shopping and dinner trips in the city like the one he thought she was on with friends tonight. Earlier, she had called Tom to tell him she drank one too many glasses of wine and would be spending the night at her friend Winnie's house. She knew that Tom didn't like Winnie, so it was unlikely that he would call to check up on her.

"Sir," Lillian said to Michael. That will be $325, plus room tax. How will you be paying today?"

Without thinking, Michael snapped his credit card down on the counter. But before Lillian could collect it, he covered it with his hand. He hadn't thought about how he would explain a charge this large on the credit card bill. "Hold on a minute, please. Do you have a cash machine here?"

She understood. Lillian nodded and pointed to an alcove across from the elevator bank.

"I'll be right back." He stepped away from the desk and indicated to Karen that he was going to the cash machine. She smiled and mouthed that she was going to use the ladies' room just off of the lobby.

She closed the stall door, placed her purse on the fold-down purse shelf, and reached into it. On her way to meet Michael for dinner, she stopped at Victoria's Secret and purchased a new, sexy pair of panties for the occasion. She unwrapped the black, lacey underwear and used her teeth to remove the tag. She hiked up her skirt and started to pull down the panties that she had put on earlier in the day. Lifting one foot off the floor, she lost her balance and slammed into the enormous toilet paper holder, shaking the wall and sending her purse to the floor, her lipstick rolling out of her reach. She righted herself and stood still for a minute, listening. Had anyone heard the thud? It would have been embarrassing. Phew. Nothing. She was alone. She tried again, sitting down on the toilet this time. She removed her panties over her sandals, and then pulled on the new pretty panties. She stood up again, making sure not to tuck her skirt into them. *Oh my god*, she thought. *I've seen too many sitcoms.*

Because Karen was already feeling guilty about what she was about to do, and even though no one else was in the ladies' lounge, she flushed the toilet to make it appear that her reason for being in there was valid. She opened the door and searched the floor and picked up her lipstick and any other items that had fallen out of her purse. As she washed her hands, she looked in the mirror. She laughed then whispered to herself, *What am I doing?* She shook her head and went back to the lobby.

Michael walked to the lobby sofa, where Karen was sitting.

"Can we just sit here for a minute before we go up to the room and . . . you know . . ."

"Sure, Karen, anything you want." He sat down next to her.

"What did you tell Alisa?" Karen asked Michael about his wife. "I mean, where did you say you would be tonight?"

"Oh, um," He was surprised by the question. "I just said I had a dinner meeting that would probably run late." He stopped to think for a minute. His wife Alisa had been very understanding and even packed an overnight bag for him, suggesting that if his meeting ended late, he should stay overnight at an inexpensive hotel rather than drive all the way home.

"Is this the right thing to do? I mean, dinner is one thing, but sex is another. I feel guilty enough."

"Guilty?" Michael asked. "Why? Oh my god, you even ordered a small salad for dinner at one of the most romantic restaurants in the city." He smiled and tried to lighten the mood. "I ingest more roughage if I mow the lawn with my mouth open."

"But Michael, this isn't… I don't do this type of thing."

"What type of thing? Finally accepting that we love each other and putting *our* needs first?"

Wait a minute—love? Karen was shocked. True, she was attracted the Michael and had fantasized about what it would be like to have him touch her, kiss her, and be inside of her, but she never considered love. Had she led him to believe that she loved him? Lust yes, desire yes, fantasies definitely but not love.

"Listen," he looked at the key card in his hand. "Let's go up to the room. We'll have a glass of wine and relax." He pointed to the bag of leftovers and joked, "And if we get hungry . . ."

"Can I ask you a question, Michael?" She was stalling. "Have you done this before?"

He hesitated. "No, I haven't." He wasn't convincing. "This is strange for me too. After all, Tom is my friend but . . ."

"But what?" Karen was looking for a reason or an excuse to end the affair before it began.

"I don't think it's a secret Karen, that Tom hasn't been faithful to you . . ." He realized how manipulative he sounded. Even he knew that was a low blow.

"Do I?" Karen was suddenly offended. "Tom's fidelity is my issue to deal with. It's not yours. My guess is that you have your hands full, too." She was becoming argumentative. Perhaps she was trying to justify a reason to bail out of the evening. "I'm sorry, Michael. I didn't mean to snap at you. I'm just nervous."

"That's okay. I know you're nervous, I am too. I think it's important that we allow ourselves to experience our emotions. I know it sounds crazy, but I believe that we need to be open to what the universe has planned for us."

As they approached the elevators Karen stopped dead in her tracks. "You do know that there's no turning back once this happens. It will have happened and we won't be able to rewrite history. Social events will probably be uncomfortable, and it won't take long for Tom and Alisa to catch on." Karen recalled the sunscreen display and how that split second made her heart ache. "Are you willing to risk your marriage for this? Have we thought this through? I have to tell you, I'm not a good liar."

"So would you tell Tom?" Michael swallowed hard.

"I said I'm not a good liar." She looked at Michael and grinned. "I didn't say I was a crazy." She slipped her hand in his.

"Are you ready?" Michael asked.

Their conversation was interrupted by a loud exchange across the lobby. "What's this? You suddenly have a con-science?" The woman yelled as they exited the elevator. "After years of sneaking around in hotels and sneaking a fuck in bathrooms and backyards, today . . . you feel bad?" She was punishing someone and she didn't care who heard it. She should have cared. When she looked up, her husband Michael was standing twenty feet away.

All of the color left Alisa's face. Tom followed her gaze. Next to his best friend Michael stood his own wife Karen.

Michael immediately let go of his grip on Karen's hand. "Oh no, Karen, I'm so sorry."

Alisa stopped breathing for a second. She and Tom had been caught. Her mind was working a mile a minute. How did Michael and Karen find out? Did they follow them to the hotel? Had they known all along? *Oh God,* she thought *he's going to divorce me and throw me out on to the street.*

Michael stepped forward and looked Alisa in the eyes, "Where are the kids?"

"They're with your moth—" She stopped herself. "Wait a minute. What are *you* two doing here?" It was coming together. Michael was supposedly at a dinner meeting and Karen . . . Well, Alisa had never seen Karen wear makeup before. She glared at Karen, "Are you fucking my husband?" Then she looked at Michael, "I overestimated you. I would've thought you had better taste in women."

Tom's jaw dropped, "That's enough from you." He stepped away from her. She had been right—they were not nice people.

Tears were forming in Michael's eyes as he looked up at Tom. "Tom," he tried. "I know it won't help, but I'm sorry. This," he indicated Karen and himself, "This is my fault. I convinced Karen to meet me. This is the first . . ."

"Thanks Tom, but no." Karen shook her head then looked at Michael, "I came here tonight because I wanted to. Not to hurt you, but for my own selfish reasons. *You* of all people should understand that."

Alisa interrupted and asked sarcastically, "And, where is my apology?"

"Don't hold your breath for an apology from me." Michael snapped at her. An apology seemed like the least important bit of minutia to deal with at the moment.

Everyone was caught in the act. They all stood there motionless and speechless.

"I supposed this is what you call a stalemate." In an effort to rationalize the moment, Michael did what he did best; as a motivational speaker, he tried to justify any uneasiness. "Let's face it. We are all surprised. We are all guilty. We are all embarrassed. We are all angry. We are not going to solve any of this standing in a hotel lobby. So what should we do?" He asked, but it was a rhetorical question. "I don't care how mad or sad you are, you simply have to laugh. The improbability of this happening here tonight is astronomical. Yet we managed it. There are twenty-four hours in a day, and 365 days in a year, and what? There must be hundreds of hotels, motels, and inns in this city. We need to ask ourselves why and how did this come together, right here, right now to uncover the hypocrisies of our marriages? This is what you call kismet."

He continued. "I'll say it. It happened because it was supposed to happen. Whether we fix our problems or go our own separate ways, we all have something in common. No matter how unpleasant, this ties us together. We're four adults, who for some reason are unkind, disloyal, or immoral. We are each going to have to come to terms with our behavior, but as I've said, we are not going to solve any of this tonight. So I say let's just take a moment to congratulate ourselves and each other on reaching this precipice. So with that said," he concluded, "I think we should go to the bar, get a drink, and make a toast to ourselves."

Michael's proclamation was followed by silence. Alisa looked at Karen. Karen looked at Tom. Tom looked at Alisa. Then they all looked at Michael.

"Do people pay you for that advice?" Tom was amazed.

Karen chimed in. "Let me understand this. So what you're saying is now that we have all been exposed as adulterers, we should hold hands and sing 'Kumbaya'?"

"Well," Michael shook his head and smiled. "We don't have to sing. That would be silly. Maybe we could all just take a deep, cleansing breath together." He inhaled deeply, pulling his hands up in front of him and then pushed them outward as he exhaled.

Alisa just shook her head. She looked at her husband then said, "I think I can speak for Tom and Karen when I say, 'bullshit!' That may be the dumbest thing I have ever heard." She pulled her keys out of her purse and looked at Tom and Karen. "Who needs a ride home?"

THE LOBBY

"Oh man, Mr. Pasternak. Did you see that?" Charlie asked. He walked around in front of Oscar and waited for an answer. He looked at Mr. Pasternak, but his eyes were closed. The dinner that had been delivered to him was untouched.

Charlie wasn't going to fall for this trick again. When he patted him on the shoulder and said, "Nice try, Oscar," Oscar fell forward.

"Come on, Mr. Pasternak, enough is enough. Here," he grasped the old man's shoulder to help him up, but there was no response. He swallowed hard and then gently shook Mr. Pasternak's shoulder again. Again, there wasn't a response. He shook him a little harder and Oscar fell forward a little more. Charlie began to panic.

"Oh my god," he whispered to himself, "What do I do? What do I do?" He looked around. Vicky and Connie had gone on a break together. He was on his own.

"Jenny," he whispered as loud as he could and waved her over. "Go call the paramedics. Tell them that one of our guests has died." He nodded toward Oscar Pasternak, "I think it's real this time. I'm pretty sure he's not breathing. Really." Charlie look scared. "Please be discrete. We don't want to worry the other guests."

Charlie lifted Oscar back into the chair and sat down next to him. He started thinking about the conversations he had with Oscar but couldn't recall if he mentioned any children or relations. *It's sort of sad*, Charlie thought as he looked around, *to die alone in a hotel lobby.*

Jenny walked over. "I made the call. The paramedics should be here in two to five minutes." She looked at poor Mr. Pasternak. "This is terrible."

"Well," Charlie tried to comfort Jenny, "Despite how it ended, I think he had a good day today. He read his paper, watched some of the crazy guests come and go, met new

157

people, watched a wedding, and saw his old friend Jacqueline."
He swallowed hard. "Oh, how are we going to tell her?"

Although Charlie wasn't a religious person, he decided to
offer a quiet prayer while he sat with Oscar's body until the
paramedics arrived. He and Jenny joined hands. "I enjoyed
our time together, Mr. Pasternak. I wish I had gotten to
know you better. I hope you rest in peace. Good-bye, Oscar."

"Gotcha!" Mr. Pasternak jumped up.

"Oh fuck!" Charlie put his hand over his heart. "I hate
you, Oscar!"

"Don't count me out yet. Oh, how I wish you had been
on the Academy Awards nominating committee." He laughed
as he stood up and picked up his tray. "I'll see you tomorrow.
I've got to get my beauty rest. My agent set up a brunch
meeting for me tomorrow. It's some fan or young film
student. Who knows anymore?" He walked away shaking his
head, "Rest in peace. Ha!"

10:00 P.M.

The shrilling sound was so loud, so piercing, so cringe-worthy and skin crawling that it made fingernails on a chalk-board sound like spa music. Maurice the doorman winced and hunched his shoulders for the twenty seconds it took for it to stop. He tried to shake the sound out of his head. He even ran his tongue across his teeth. He wanted to make sure his caps had not cracked. The sound was made by the brakes of a large, shiny bus as it pulled up and stopped in front of the hotel doors. The side panels of the bus were painted with the name "Most Happy Sunshine Tours." Alongside the lettering was a cartoonish picture of an orange and yellow smiling sun that was ironically wearing sunglasses. There was also a picture of a winking surfboard with arms and a hand posi-tioned in an "okay" gesture. Around the neck of the human-ized surfboard hung a camera.

Instantaneously, as soon as the bus completed its stop, there was a flurry of activity inside of it. Though it's tinted windows, the doorman could see the passengers spring from their seats and bags and packages were being pulled down from the overhead compartments. Maurice moved quickly over to the valet desk, grabbed the phone, and dialed "11."

"Front desk," Lillian answered the phone with a smile. "How may I help you?"

"Hello, Miss Lillian. This is Moe, at the door." Lillian looked up and waved. Her smile faded when she looked beyond Moe and focused on the load of people exiting the bus. "Brace yourself, Miss Lillian. Here comes the Most Happy Sunshine tour group."

Within minutes, dozens of tourists poured out onto the sidewalk. As the driver and his assistant opened the luggage compartments and started unloading the baggage, the hotel's valets grabbed their rolling carts and ran out to meet them.

A little man wearing a small, brimmed fisherman's cap with Chinese lettering on the front worked desperately to rein in the crowd. He made a hand motion which indicated that he wanted them to stay put while he went inside the hotel to secure their accommodations.

"Excuse prease." The small man with a very heavy accent begged as he approached the reception desk. Our prane was derayed," he bowed. He looked at his clipboard. "I am a-supposed to speak with a Miss Ho, the a-cuss-omer re-ae-zon.

"Oh yes, Heidi, Heidi Ho, the customer liaison. Yes. She has stepped away from the desk for a moment. I'm Lillian Levine," she chirped and tapped her name tag. "How may I help you?"

"A Rirrian Revine?" he bowed, "I prease wait for Miss Ho. However, I thank you a-very much."

"Nî hâo, wô de míngzì shì Heidi Ho. Huànyíng wô hên lèyì bàngzhù nî," Heidi said to the man as she walked up. She then whispered to Lillian, "I said hello and that I would be happy to help him."

"We will use Engrish in United States," He smiled sweetly. "I am Misser Kim from Mos Happy Sunshiny Tour Bus. I bereave we have a-reservason for ereven single room and twenty fwee a-double room."

"Yes, Mister Kim, your English is very good. Please wait a minute while I check-in your group."

"A-scews me Miss a-Ho." Mister Kim asked. "Are you a-Chinese? You appear to speak fruentry, but you have a-brond hair and you don't rook a-Chinese." He seemed interested.

"Oh yes, Mister Kim. I am half Chinese and half German." She explained, "My father was an international businessman from China when he met my mother, who was an innkeeper in the town call Meissen, on the River Elbe in Germany. Have you heard of it?" She continued, "Dad regularly visited Meissen to buy fine porcelains for his clients and every time he was there, he stayed at that hotel where my mother worked. Eventually, he and my mother fell in love and got married. His business took them around the world and they eventually settled down in the United States to raise a family. I don't know, Mr. Kim," she said dreamily, "maybe because it's such a romantic story, it made me want to work in the hotel business." She smiled sweetly and shrugged.

When Mister Kim stepped away to organize his group, Lillian walked over to Heidi. stunned, she asked, "I never knew that about you. Is that true?"

Heidi laughed, "Hell no. But it's fun to tell the story. You'd be amazed at how many people believe it." She shook her head. "I studied Mandarin in college as part of my international business degree. My last name is really Horowitz. But c'mon, Heidi Horowitz? It hardly rings of "international woman of intrigue," so I shortened it to 'Ho.'" She laughed, "My parents are Paula and Myron Horowitz from the San Fernando Valley. And my hair? Oh, it's L'Oreal Superior Preference. I was trying for highlights but got carried away. And now . . ." She posed, "I'm a blond Ho."

Lillian helped Heidi print the keycards and make the room assignments according to the Most Happy Sunshine tour roster. The group moved as a unit through the doors, jamming ten and twelve people in to each of the revolving door wings. There was no pushing, no shoving, just perfect synchronization. It could be an Olympic event.

"Here you go, Mister Kim. I have double keys for each room." She motioned to the bellmen. "Mr. Kim, these bellmen will be helping your group up to their rooms. Please let me know if you need anything else. Wân ân."

Suddenly Heidi's attention was drawn to a ruckus in the lobby, near the doors. It was Minnie, a known street person who regularly stopped in at the Shipley to either get warm, use the restrooms, or sing and dance for money. However, on each and every occasion, she was quickly escorted out of the building.

Although she hated having to do it, Heidi had to call Joe, one of the security officers on duty, and ask him to discretely and gently escort Minnie out of the building. Although harmless and certainly more than a little entertaining, the sight and sound of a raggedy homeless person singing bawdy tunes in the lobby of a premier hotel was upsetting to the guests.

"Do me a favor, Joe," Heidi handed him a five-dollar bill. "Give this to her."

As Joe walked toward her, Minnie sidestepped and shimmied away from him while she sang:

Gather 'round, all ye whorey!
Gather 'round and hear my story!
When a man grows old, and his balls grow cold,
And the tip of his prick turns blue,
Far from a life of Yukon strife,
He can tell you a tale or two.
So pull up a seat, and buy me one neat
And a tale to you I will tell,
About Dead-Eye Dick and Mexican Pete,
And a harlot named Eskimo Nell.

"Come on, Minnie, you've gotta go." Joe took her by the arm.

"Oh, I understand Joe, I do. But I wanted to share one of my favorite ditties with the folks." As Joe took her out the front doors, she hollered behind her, "That was the 'Ballad of Eskimo Nell.' I hope you liked it. My next show is at eleven."

"What the hell was that?" Charlie caught the end of Minnie's floor show.

"Oh that's Minnie. She calls herself Minnie the Moocher," Heidi answered. "She's harmless. Sometimes she just wants some attention and a few dollars," Heidi smiled, "but she's always willing to sing or dance for it. I like her."

One rainy night when the lobby was empty Heidi had asked Minnie about her life. Minnie told an extraordinary story. "When she was a young woman, about sixty years ago," Heidi explained to Charlie, "Minnie was the lead dancer at one of the clubs on Broadway. She said she was a stripper, and apparently she had quite a large following. So I looked her up on the Internet, and you know what? She *was* famous." Heidi raised her hands in front of her as if she were reading a marque, "She was known as the 'Red Hot Hoochie Coocher.'"

"So what happened? How did she end up on the street? It's so sad."

"Not for Minnie," Heidi said, still staring at the door. "She gave all of her money away to charity. She said it complicated her life. She said it made her pretentious."

"Speaking of pretentious," Charlie nodded in the direction of Double D and his lame-looking entourage as they entered the lobby from the elevator, preparing to depart for an evening of "par-tay-ing."

Suddenly there was an eruption of activity among the Chinese tour group. "Is-a Daba Dee! Is-a Daba Dee!" A Most

Happy Sunshine tourist waved her friends over. "Isa Missa Dada Dee from teravision." They swarmed around him.

"Oh Missa Daba Dee, I your fan." One woman said as she took a selfie with him. "May I prease have your asignatu here?" She pointed to her breast and handed him a pen.

"See," he beamed as he said to his entourage. "I've still got it."

◆ ◆

Francis LaPorte's shift was over. He collected his duffle bag from the backroom and was headed to the restroom when Lillian stopped him. "Before you leave, Francis," she asked, "would you mind stopping back at the desk? I'll need you to show Charlie how to clock out and explain how to fill in his timecard."

Francis nodded, "I'll be back in a few minutes. I just have to change."

Charlie looked at Lillian. "Really? Don't you think I know how to clock out? Besides, I don't think Francis likes me."

"Oh, you don't know anything about Francis." Lillian smiled and explained, "I think he'll surprise you."

Five, then ten, then twenty minutes passed and Charlie looked at his watch again. "Lillian, I thought I was supposed to meet with Francis. Do you think he forgot about me? I'm hungry and I would like to go home." He was impatient. "How much longer do I need to wait?"

"Oh, I think he'll be here in a minute." She looked up and saw a woman dressed in formal wear approaching the desk. "Why don't you help this guest? I'm sure Francis will be here before you know it."

Charlie looked up and saw a beautiful woman approaching. She was tall and slender and dressed in a sparkly, formfitting evening gown and long, white gloves. Her gown had a slit up the middle from her ankles, ending just low enough to cover what Charlie could only imagine were a pair of lacey panties. Charlie looked around expecting to see a refined gentleman wearing a tuxedo to accompany her, ready to whisk her off for an elegant late supper or, maybe a nightcap.

The woman looked like she could be a movie star. He tried to recall. Had any celebrities checked in? Not that he could remember. But they usually used false names, anyway. He laughed to himself when he thought about that Double D character and how he ended up being a celebrity to the tour group.

The woman was tall like Gina Davis or Mandy Moore; she had dark, long hair, her makeup was perfect, and she had full ruby-colored lips and a lot of flashy jewelry. She glided up to the front desk and looked directly at Charlie who swallowed hard.

"Well," she said in a deep, gravelly voice. "Are you ready?"

"Yes, ma'am." Charlie's eyes opened wide. He leaned forward, looked around and whispered, "Ready for what?"

She rolled her eyes and placed her purse on the counter. "I thought you needed help with you timecard. Didn't you need me to show you how to clock out?"

Wait, what? Charlie's mouth dropped open, "Francis? Is that you?"

"Of course it's me," Francis looked at the delicate watch which was on *her* begloved wrist. "Do you mind if we get right to it? I have an engagement and I don't want to be late."

Lillian walked up behind Charlie. "I didn't realize you had plans, Franny. You go ahead, don't be late. I'll take care of it." She added, "Oh, by the way, you look beautiful. Is that a new dress?"

Francis smiled and stepped back for Lillian to see. "Don't you love it? I got it on sale at Loehmann's."

11:00 P.M.

"Is there anything we need to know?" Gina pointed at Bella and back at herself when she asked Lillian Levine about shift change information.

"Nope," Lillian smiled then looked toward the ballroom then the bar, "the high school reunion should be wrapping up soon. We just checked in a tour group, the bar is still going strong, and . . ." she looked at a note she had written, "there's a late check-in for the Kreitz party. But that's about it. Have a good night."

They readied their work area. Because there is less guest traffic during the late shift, the desk staff usually had some data entry to do. The lobby was quiet and could be lonely during the wee hours, but over the years of working together Gina and Bella had become best friends. "After all," Gina would say, "other than a vampire, who else could be our friend?"

"So, G," Bella asked. "Did you get that problem taken care of at home?"

"Oh yeah, my mother-in-law . . ." she rolled her eyes. "Yup, she has officially moved herself into my house. So now she saves on bus fair and doesn't have to burst an aneurysm while waiting to insult me about my housekeeping and mothering skills. Now she'll be there all of the time. It's really much more convenient for her. As you know, that's what I live for." Gina sniffed. "On the upside, she does the laundry and watches the kids while Jim's at work and I'm napping." Gina pulled a tissue from her pocket and dabbed her eyes. "Can you smell that?"

Bella leaned in. "Let me smell? It smells like powder aaa ... and ... ah, bug repellant? What *is* that?"

"I know," Gina nodded. "I'm allergic to my underwear now. She puts some sort of industrial-strength fabric softener in the wash. It keeps me from chaffing, and I suppose I no longer have to worry about those pesky vermin that live in my drawers but I am nearly asphyxiated every time I put on my underpants."

Bella laughed. "Maybe if I bring some of my laundry over, she can help me keep some of the pests I know from trying to get into my pants."

Gina handed Bella a stack of papers and then asked, "I thought you were dating someone. Isn't that working out?"

"Frankly, I'm about to give up." She looked out into the lobby. "I can't seem to find anyone who has any idea how to treat a lady," she shrugged.

Deb and Susan walked hand in hand through the lobby after a full day of sightseeing. It had been such a long time since they had held each other's hand. Who knew the reason why they had stopped in the first place? After ten years, had they become complacent? Was it a reaction, a defense mechanism after enduring a decade's worth of sideways glances or grumbled comments from homophobes or jealous gay people? Today none of that mattered. Today it felt good.

"Oh, Deb, I had such a wonderful day. We have to make a point of saving our money so we can go on more vacations like this one." She giggled then made an affected pouty face and joked, "I can't believe I lost my new scarf."

Deb laughed and held up Sue's hand then twirled underneath. "I would have loved to have stayed at the club and danced some more, but I got tired of being knocked and jostled around the dance floor. It's funny. That never used to bother me. I guess I'm getting old, huh?"

"No, we're not old, we just don't have that superhuman, turbo-party strength anymore. Remember? We used to start our weekends at four o'clock on Friday afternoon ..."

"Yeah," Sue picked up her train of thought, "and powered only by pizza, cocktail nut mix, and well drinks, we'd dance our last dance late Sunday evening. Then," she widened her eyes, "we'd pop out of bed on Monday morning, fresh and ready to go to work. That was crazy."

"I think coffee was stronger back then." Deb kissed the back of Sue's hand.

"Honey," Susan squeezed Deb's hand, "let's try to remember to hold hands more often. I really miss it."

"Me too, Suz," she squeezed back. "You know what?" She stopped walking. "I don't really want the day to end. Can we go to the hotel bar?" Deb smiled mischievously, "I hear music and I think I'm getting a second wind."

The smell of old gym shoes and mold preceded Joe Kreitz as he followed the valet who was rolling his sample case into the lobby. Joe Kreitz—who was also known as Mister Cheeses and The Lord of Cheese—was in town to meet with west coast grocery buyers. A lovable guy, Joe was all business when it came to cheese. "Cheese," he would say, "is a religious experience, and I am the lord of cheese. Call me 'Cheeses Krietz.'"

Joe visited the area three or four times a year to promote his company, The Kreitz Family Cheesery's bounty to the west coast grocery store chains. "You can't smell cheese over the phone or in an email. Ya just gotta taste it," he'd say.

"Hi, Mr. Cheeses," Gina beamed. She had just settled into her shift when she saw Mr. Krietz walk through the door. She knew it was going to be a good night. She loved when he visited. He was an older gentleman who was always so spirited—well, corny. Rounder than he was tall, he managed to find high-water pants for his shorter-than-short legs. The waistband of his slacks was always folded over and the bottom button of his shirt was losing the battle with its button hole. And it was as if he chose the most ill-fitting toupee he could find: a style that would look better on a man with *some* hair, you know, a sort of horseshoe around the sides of his head. But Mr. Cheeses' toupee looked like a hair island, floating on a sea of flesh. Gina figured that because he was so loveable, no one had the heart to tell him.

Joe would practically throw a clot trying to come up with cheese-related puns. It didn't matter what time of day he arrived. It was always a fun experience. "Hey, Mr. Kreitz," Gina cleared her throat. "It's Gouda see you again."

"That's a good one, Gina." He smiled. "Well, I've gained some weight." He patted his belly. "I keep getting feta. See how I did that? I switched feta for fatter . . ." Mr. Cheeses had a habit of explaining all of his puns. It was hilarious, and certainly funnier than the puns themselves.

He smiled, winked, and offered what she had been waiting for, "I see you Gruyère." He pointed at her head. "Get it? Get it? See how I did that with Gruyère and 'grew your hair?'"

I do, Mister Kreitz..." she was stopped by him, "I mean, Mister Cheeses. We're happy to have you here again."

"To be honest, Gina, I wanted to stay at The Stilton, but it was full. Get it? You see what I did with the Stilton, the Hilt—."

After a minute, Gina came around the desk and whispered, "Oh, Mr. Cheeses, I'm afraid to tell you that something is . . ." she paused and waved her hand in front of her nose, "is very ripe." She pointed at his sample case.

"I know, unfortunately. I'm afraid a hooligan left the case out on the runway a bit too long before loading it onto the airplane. I hope I haven't made this trip in 'blue vein.'" He winked, "Get it? You see what I did there . . ." he laughed, "Well, they can't all be winners." Without a thought, but with much effort, he crouched down and unlatched the case. As he swung it open, the smell nearly knocked Gina over. She had to steady herself with the back of the sofa. "I'll go call the kitchen right now, and have them find a place in the refrigerators for you."

"Thanks Gina, everyone knows that you simply can't have a meeting without samples, it would be a Limburger of ideas."

Joe walked around the couch and looked at Hank who was still waiting for Mary Margaret. "What's the matter with you? Or as the Roquefort said to the Gorgonzola, Why so blue?"

"I'm not. I'm just waiting for my wife. She's late." He looked at his watch again.

"You seem worried."

"Nah," Hank was tired. "It's just . . . you know."

"I do. You can't live with 'em, and you'd go to jail . . . never mind." Joe patted Hank on the back. "Like I always say, 'marriage is like cheese. Sometimes it's nutty, funky and complex, sometimes it has a gentle sweetness, and sometimes it just stinks. But it's always better with wine.' How about it if I buy you a glass of chardonnay? It's on me. They're playing music in the bar. It think it's R & Brie."

"I said no."

"You can't tell me you didn't feel something," a pudgy man wearing a Master Flash tag whined as he followed Florentine Moretti, the very serious, very annoyed administrative assistant through the lobby. "What was with all that provocative dancing?" He tried to negotiate.

"That wasn't provocative, Peter. When you pushed your crotch against me, I stumbled."

He sped up and was right behind her. "Listen, I know you're worried about the fact that I'm married, but like I've said, my wife and I have an understanding. We have an open marriage, so it's cool."

Florentine stopped dead in her tracks and turned around. "Is it? Is it really?" She held out her hand. "Then give me your cellphone, Peter. I'm gonna call your wife and ask her."

He reached for it, but then stopped. He knew better. "Um, the battery is dead."

"Fine," she walked over to the front desk and asked Gina, "May I use your phone, please?" She turned around. "Peter, what is your wife's phone number?"

"Bitch." He said it under his breath but she heard it.

"That's what I thought." She turned to Gina and said, "Isn't it funny how I'm 'hot' and 'the girl of his dreams' until I say no, then I'm a bitch." She thought for a moment, then turned back toward Peter. "I don't want you think I'm a bitch, so I'll tell you what . . . I'll consider it." She looked him straight in the eye and continued, "Just show it to me, right now. I've got to see what I'm workin' with."

"What?" Peter was confused.

"Yeah, show me your dick, and . . ." she looked over at Gina, "what's your name?"

"Gina, ma'am." And from behind her, Belle raised her hand, "I'm Belle."

As this was occurring, Donny, the very flamboyant and affected gay bar-back who had come to the desk to get some change interrupted them, "Belle, I need some ones, please." He stopped and looked at the scene. "Hey bitches, what's going on?"

Gina filled him in, "We're going to look at this man's penis to see if it worth it for this lady to sleep with him."

"Ooh," Donny clapped his hands together, "I am very good at this type of thing." He looked at Florentine, "I want to help."

"Great, okay." Florentine turned back toward Peter and summarized, "So, Gina and Belle and . . ."

"Donny, my name is Donny."

"Right, so Gina, Belle, and Donny and I will see if it's worth it. So go ahead, pull it out." She folded her arms across her chest. "I don't know what you're worried about. You've been talking about it all night."

She looked past Peter and saw a small group of soft, pale, middle-aged people walk into the lobby. They were carrying glow sticks and wearing pointy hats, capes, and other glittery paraphernalia. It looked as if they were returning from some comic-bookish witch and warlock convention. "I want to be fair, Peter. You can pick some of your own judges, too." She indicated to the group that was now standing at the entrance, mesmerized by the wizardry of the lobby's magical revolving door. "Looks like you might have a chance to swing the vote with that group on your side."

Peter held up his hands. "Fine, I get it. You've made your point." He turned around to walk away.

Hank, who was still sitting on the lobby sofa waiting for his wife, had overheard the whole exchange. "Women," he shrugged, "they're like cheese."

12:00 A.M.

At midnight, Peggy stumbled into the lobby of the hotel, her pleather purse hanging in front of her from her neck, her shoes in hand. She didn't notice Hank who was sitting on a lobby sofa as she headed into the bar.

"Bar-friender, I'll have an Irish coffee, please," she slurred as she climbed on to a cushioned barstool. For a minute, she watched Deb and Sue sitting at the end of the bar. Sitting with fingers intertwined and gazing into each other's eyes, they appeared to be entranced by one another. Being a little tipsy Peggy interrupted anyhow. "Excuse me ladies, may I say that I envy how you look at one another. It's so romantic. Trust me," She tapped her own chest with her finger, "you need to find a way to keep feeling that way about each other. I'll bet you girls like to do the same things."

"Not always," Sue smiled and nudged Deb. "But we try to compromise."

"Where the heck have you been, Mary Margaret?" Hank came up to her from behind. He startled her.

"Peggy! My name is Peggy, or Peg or Meg, anything but Mary Margaret. It sounds like I'm a reverend mother, for God's sake. I think after thirty-five years you could drop the formality and be my friend. After all, you *have* seen me naked." She winked at Deb and Sue.

"Mary Margaret!" he was shocked. "What has come over you?" Hank admonished her.

She ignored his tone. "I have been out and about in San Francisco, having the time of my life. You should have been there Hank. I saw an exhibit at the Modern Art Museum. Then I went to have a late lunch, but . . ." She lost track of what she was saying when her Irish coffee was set in front of her. "And . . . oh yeah! The restaurant where I was going to eat lunch was getting ready for dinner and wasn't seating anyone in the dining room, but the bar was open. So, I sat in the bar and I said to myself 'hey, why not?'" She made an exaggerated shrug. "So, I ordered a glass of Chablis and some fried something–or–another." She giggled, "Oh my goodness, Hank. I think I ate squid or octopus. It was like eating rubber bands." She slapped the bar with her hand. "It was a hoot!"

"Oh, so now you're a drinker?" Hank folded his arms across his chest.

She glared at him then continued. "I met up with a couple of nice gals. I'd say they were in their thirties. They were on vacation, and can you believe it? They left their husbands at home! They were on their own." She took a deep breath in and exhaled. "Well," she said, "we got to chatting and they bought me another glass of wine. We were having such a good time that after a while they invited me to join them at this place called Buena Vista." She sipped her drink. "Hank," she slapped his arm, "that's where Irish coffee was invented. And boy! It was delicious! Well," she continued, "while we were there, a few more of their girlfriends showed up. And guess what?" She didn't wait for Hank to guess. "They insisted that I go to dinner with them. 'Well,' I said to myself, 'since I'm having such a good time . . .'"

"Didn't you even think about me and where I might be? Did you think I might want to have dinner?" Hank tried to take charge of the conversation.

"I did," she paused, "for a minute. But then I remembered you were following 'your plan.' Besides, I just knew that you would *want* me to have a good time. Don't you want me to have a good time, Hank?" She playfully looked out of the corner of her eye.

No! "Of course I do, but . . ."

"That's what I thought. So, I went." Peggy finished her coffee drink in a gulp and motioned to the bartender to set her up with another. "Oh, have one, Hank. You'll love it."

"Caffeine? At his hour?"

"He'll have his made with decaf," she instructed the barman then turned to Hank. "I learned something today, Hank. I learned that I need to have some fun in my life, not a regimented series of drills and tasks. That's not living, it's just existing." She patted his hand. "It's not your fault, Hank. I was lazy. I let you tell me what to do and how to do it. But I don't want to do that anymore." She clumsily stood up and saluted. "You are relieved of your duties sir."

Hank looked shocked. "You're drunk." He tried to dismiss her behavior.

"So what, Hank. So what if I had a few—no, several—cocktails. Perhaps you should loosen up too." She pushed is decaf Irish coffee toward him.

". . . And," she continued, "if you don't want to have fun with me, then I'm going to do it on my own."

"You didn't even call, or . . ." Hank realized that he had lost control.

"I love you, Hank. I really do. But if I don't start having some fun, I may just crack. You can join me if you want to, and I hope you do, but if you don't, I'm sorry . . . No," she corrected herself. "No, I'm not sorry. But I'm just going to do it without you. I hope you understand."

"Mary Margaret—um, Peggy. I was . . ."

"Hank? Were you truly worried? Or were you angry that I wasn't falling into line?" She knew the answer and it didn't really matter. She had gotten a reaction rather than direction from him. It was a good first step. "Hank, honey, would you do me a favor?"

He seemed wounded. "Okay, what is it?"

"Would you sit down next to me?" she patted the bar-stool. "Try this Irish coffee, and let's talk about extending our trip a day or two and doing something that we both want to do," she added, "together."

"Hey Curt, my man, I should have known you'd be in the bar." Tripp Matthews, Curt's mentor, stepped up and slapped him on the back. "What are you doing wading in the koi pond when we have big game to conquer?"

Curt was chatting with other Master Flash employees, most of them females. "I was just saying good-night."

"Are you kidding me?" Tripp nodded in the direction of the company's president, Joselyn Rydell. "The night is young."

"That's true, but she's talking to someone." He shook his head, "I spoke to her earlier and she didn't take the bait. I think I should lay low for a while."

"I hear ya. I'm pretty tired anyway. Phew, last night was wild." Tripp was fishing, hoping that Curtis would ask him what happened.

Without prompting a reaction from Curt, Tripp launched into a story of how he "bagged" Meredith Springer, the company's vice president, the night before. "It wasn't too difficult," he said, "of course, she recognized me. Toward the end of the "welcome" cocktail party she pulled me aside and wanted to talk about sales and my technique, then . . ." Tripp smirked and winked, "one thing led to another and before I knew it, she had her hands in my pants. We hardly made it to my room. I swear we must have done it five or six times, she didn't leave until six this morning. She's a freak, man." He held up his hand for a high five. "By any chance did you see how rough she looked when she walked into the meeting this morning?" He put his finger to his lips. "Remember bud, it has to be kept on the down-low. No one can know. But don't be surprised if you see my title change to *director of sales.*"

Curtis was speechless. Tripp was lying. It was impossible for Tripp to have slept with Meredith, because he was with her from until she slipped out of his room at around five in the morning. While listening to Tripp prattle on about his fictitious conquest, Curtis realized that he was a phony, and worse, a scandalmonger. What else had he lied about? At that moment, Curt knew that being associated with Tripp would just mean trouble for him. "You know what, Tripp?" he paused and chose his words carefully, "I've got to hand it to you, man. Your story is absolutely unbelievable. I have a lot to learn."

Knowing now that Tripp was all talk—and a jerk, but harmless—Curt pointed out Joselyn who was sitting with another woman at the bar, "Go for it, man. She's out of my league." He crossed his arms, "I'll just stand back and watch you work."

"Alright then," Tripp swallowed hard, straightened his shirt cuffs and then walked over to where the ladies were sitting. He couldn't let down his mentee.

"Hello ladies, I'm Tripp Matthews. May I buy you a drink?"

"Oh hello, Mr. Matthews." Joselyn smiled. "I've heard about you. Your friend Curtis over there mentioned you earlier when he made advances toward me." She looked past him and over his shoulder at Curtis. "Why don't you bring him over here too. I'd like to pick up where we left off." She smiled at her friend.

"Ah, oh okay." Tripp walked back to where Curtis was standing. "I don't know what you said to her earlier today, but she and her friend want you to come over there too." He pumped his fist. "We're in." Even though Curt protested, Tripp pleaded, "Don't cock block me, man." Then he grabbed Curt by the arm and pushed him over to the bar.

"Oh hi, Curt," Joselyn smiled. "I have to tell you that you made quite an impression on me earlier today. I haven't been able to stop thinking about you." She stopped herself and apologized. "Oh where are my manners? Mr. Matthews, Mr. Waters, this is Rebecca Tipton."

"How ya doing, sweetheart?" Tripp winked and positioned himself next to her, slinging his arm over the back of the tall bar chair she was sitting on. Clearly Joselyn was more interested in Curtis, but Rebecca was pretty hot too.

Joselyn took a sip from her glass of wine and continued, "Rebecca is the attorney for Master Flash. We were just chatting about sexual harassment on the job. Did you know that it can go both ways?"

"Ah . . ." Tripp's expression changed from stupidly excited to just plain stupid.

"Yes," Rebecca continued, "there have been a number of cases where an employee intentionally puts his employer in a compromising position, then he files false complaints or he attempts to set up or blackmail his employer. Then," she gave Joselyn a knowing glance, "if he doesn't get what he wants, he sues her in a quid pro quo or hostile work environment case."

"What happens then, Rebecca?" Joselyn prompted her attorney. She was having fun and the looks on the boys' faces were priceless.

"Well, Joselyn," Rebecca almost laughed, "the employee can be fired, of course."

"Well," Joselyn opened her eyes wide and agreed, "of course."

"*And* sued for legal costs." She affected a frown, "Never mind that his reputation is shot. Well," she corrected herself, "that's if he's not charged with fraud or defamation and ends up in jail."

"You know what?" Joselyn turned to look at Curtis and Tripp, "Why don't the both of you come to my office on Monday. I need to talk to you about something."

Curtis' heart dropped. He really liked his job. Why had he listened to Tripp? Curt glared at him out of the corner of his eye and Tripp swallowed hard. He knew what was coming. It happened at his past two places of employment. It was the end of the line for him. As they both slinked away Curtis whispered, "Thanks a lot, asshole."

"What?" Joselyn said to her attorney then laughed and shrugged her shoulders, "I was going to ask them to coordinate the company's annual picnic."

The Titan's class reunion party was winding down. Some of the alumni were headed to the valet stand to wait for their cars, others were headed up to their hotel rooms, and still others went to the hotel bar for a few more cocktails. After Darlene, Brad's wife left the party in a huff a few minutes earlier, Brad and Lance walked into the lobby to chat.

"Gee, man, I'm sorry I drove your wife away." Lance winked, "Did I go a little over board?"

"I think the story about the Lanceroni pizza may have just pushed her over the edge." Brad clapped his hands together with delight. "Hey, I have a question. I've been meaning to ask you. What made you decide to be a snack cake delivery person?" He shook his head, ". . . And then have a bag filled with Twinkies and Ho Hos to hand out. Man, *that* was inspired."

"Oh," Lance smiled, "Lance Cochran is a character I developed in an improvisation class. You know, he's sort of an out of touch douchebag, but he has a heart of gold. Nothing says 'I love you' like chocolates and flowers. But remember, Lance is a bit of an ass-hat, so he made romancing a 'baby-doll' with a package of cupcakes his signature move."

"Well, that was awesome. Ah, um . . ." Brad paused. "I can't believe I don't know your real name. It isn't Lance, is it?"

"Nope, it's Noah Steinberg." He held out his hand to shake Brad's. "It's nice to meet you." Noah was a student of acting at the Academy of Arts College in the city. At forty-six, after an unfulfilling career in accounting, he decided to follow his dream of becoming an actor. In an effort to make some extra cash, Noah was a contractor for a company that provided actors to do almost any acting job: be a party guest, a doting boyfriend, a clown, a butler, a chauffer, even an old high school friend.

Brad reached into his inside jacket pocket and pulled out an envelope. As he handed it to Noah he said, "Well, Noah, this is the best thousand dollars I have ever spent."

"It was a lot of fun for me too. I've never stayed in character for more than an hour or two." He appreciated the work. "Hey, Brad, do you think it will work?"

"Yes, I do," he explained. "I really do love Darlene, and I know this whole charade seems desperate, but I needed to find a way to put some excitement back into our marriage. I'm pretty sure we gave Darlene something to think about." He paused, then smiled and shook his head, "Thunder Stick? That was brilliant. You made me sound like a real stud."

"Listen, man, it was a pleasure. I had a lot of fun," Noah tugged at his pant leg, "but I have to get out of these ridiculous disco pants before little Lancelot is beheaded." Then he quoted Lance, "If you're pickin' up what I'm puttin' down."

As they walked to the elevator, Brad had one more thought. "Do you know what amazed me? During the entire reunion, no one approached or questioned you about not recognizing you from high school."

"Ha, yeah. It's amazing, isn't it? I find the key to Lance is to be so obvious and so available that I become repellant. Unfortunately, it's what happens with homeless people. Just being around Lance makes people incredibly uncomfortable and, for some strange reason, it makes some of them feel better about their own lives."

The elevator doors opened. When they looked in, Noah said, "Oh, that can't be good."

"I'll go get someone," Brad offered and ran off to the front desk.

Oscar Pasternak was lying dead on the floor of elevator number three.

1:00 A.M.

Polishing the hotel lobby's floors was a second job for Gus. He assumed people thought that the reason for this second job was that he lived beyond his means, he was deeply in debt, or that his wife relied on very expensive medications to live, but the reason was far more provocative.

Gus liked horses. Not carousel horses—he liked thoroughbred horses, the kind he could bet money on. He fancied himself quite the handicapper. He studied the horses' breeding, birth-lines, statistics, running styles, trainers, owners, and jockeys, determining which would respond to a trainer's strategy, be ridden by the most skilled jockey, or simply be the fastest in a given race, and then plan his wagers accordingly.

Gus was not in debt and his wife Maria wanted to keep it that way. Maria worked the night shift as a registered nurse at a local hospital. The night shift paid two-times what the day shift did and four-times on holidays. She was organized, nurturing, and no-nonsense. Gus loved, admired, and feared Maria all at the same time. She had created a budget which earmarked every dollar they earned, down to the penny. She insisted that their bills were paid on time, that they were saving for retirement, and that they had regular vacations and good cars. She laid down the law. "If you want to go to the horseraces and bet on the ponies, then do it with your own money." So Gus took a second job, polishing floors in the lobby of the hotel.

By day, Gus was a union plumber. It was a fine job, well-paying with benefits and security. By night he polished the floors at the Shipley Hotel. His hours were midnight to 4:00 a.m.. He made twenty-five dollars an hour, which came to five hundred per week, enough to support his hobby and bet on a few well-handicapped races each weekend.

After his regular workday, Gus would go home, have dinner with his wife, take a nap, and wake up in time for his shift at the hotel. At 11:45 p.m., Gus would arrive at the hotel, pull the polisher from the maintenance closet, and begin his shift.

The late night, early morning floor-polishing gig was perfect. Gus handicapped upcoming races while he polished the floors. The Aztec Lowrider Buffer Burnisher and its flat control panel was the perfect desk. Each night he'd lay out his Daily Racing Form on top of the Low Rider buffer and study the horses' statistics as he mindlessly ran the polisher in a figure-eight motion across the lobby's marble floor.

Just one perfect multiple race combination or obscure long shot was all he needed to finance future trips to the racetrack or into retirement.

"Hey, Gus," Belle called from the front desk. "Do you have a tip for me?"

"Yeah, sure," Gus smiled. He answered the same way every day. "Bet on the little guy with the white pants and shiny boots." It was the description of every jockey. "Do you think I'd give away the winner and lower the odds? You're out of your mind." He laughed.

Gus dreamed of hitting it big as he studied his papers and listened to the vrooming and swooshing sounds of the machine's brushes. Friday night was a perfect time to study the racing form. Feature races, jackpots, and betting incentives were usually offered by the racetracks on the weekends, which meant that the payouts would be larger. On special days, such as the Kentucky Derby or Breeders' Cup, hundreds of thousands—even tens of millions—of dollars are wagered.

Suddenly, Gus stopped dead in his tracks, shut off the polisher, and picked up his racing form to examine it more closely. He couldn't believe his eyes. He found it! The horse! A horse named Screamin' Mantra. It was a long shot in the seventh race at Saratoga Racetrack. It was what is referred to as a "maiden claiming race," which meant that the horse had never won a race (broken his maiden) and was available to be purchased (claimed) by another stable, owner, or trainer.

Screamin' Mantra was a three-year-old horse, a non-winner in any of the fourteen races he had been in. In fact, all of his performances had been pathetic. Gus put his racing form down on the buffing machine again and ran his finger across the lines of information.

All of Screamin' Mantra's past races were on the turf and had been less than a mile in distance. Although the horse looked as if he was gaining ground toward the end of each of those races, he never got closer than mid-pack. But Gus found something very interesting about Screamin' Mantra.

This race, the seventh at Saratoga, was going to be a mile and a sixteenth, and not on grass but on the dirt. Screamin' Mantra's sire was a horse named War Chant, one of Gus' favorites. And War Chant loved running longer distance races. Gus noted the horse's practices. The trainer had been practicing his horse at seven furlongs (seven-eights of a mile) and at a full mile, and *that* was basically unheard of. Most trainers practice their horses at five-eighths of a mile or less.

To Gus, it was clear that the trainer was conditioning the horse to run a further distance. He knew that when a horse was being readied to be claimed or sold, trainers rarely spent too much time training them. So seeing that this horse had been practiced and readied for this race, to Gus it meant the answer was simple. The trainer and owner didn't necessarily want him claimed, and they expected him to win and increase his value.

The morning odds for betting Screamin' Mantra were an outrageous fifty-to-one. Winning and favorite horses usually had odds of two-to-one or seven-to-five, with a payout of just four or five dollars. But fifty-to-one! A two-dollar win bet on a fifty-to-one horse would pay one hundred dollars. No one was going to bet on Screamin' Mantra—no one but Gus.

Gus pulled out his cellphone and logged into his bank account to check his balance. He had $2,041.68.

At fifty-to-one, a one-thousand-dollar bet would pay fifty thousand, and if Screamin' Mantra won, a two-thousand-dollar bet would pay one hundred thousand dollars! Gus checked his watch. He had a few hours to decide if he would invest some or all of his bankroll on Screamin' Mantra.

He spent the rest of his shift daydreaming. Would he buy a new car? Some jewelry? Would he take Maria on an exotic trip? Or would he parlay his winnings into his next big bet?

Gus the floor man smiled. As he passed by the reception desk he offered, "Quiet evening, miss."

Gina looked up. "Sure is, Gus." She added, "The floors look nice."

It was just after 1:00 a.m. and Gina, the swing-shift clerk, was preparing to review online reservation information on the computer. Just the hum of the floor-polishing machine filled the lobby.

Derek "Squeaky" Barnes stood with his eyes focused on the security monitors, and the camera feed which was catching the activity around the pool area was of special interest to him. "Squeaky" was a nickname that the night clerks gave Derek because of his crepe-soled shoes and the noise they made as he walked through the empty lobby in the wee hours of the morning. Very serious about his responsibilities as the hotel's night security officer, he roamed the halls, checking hidden vestibules and shaking door handles that led to the outside of the building.

"Wait for my word," Derek called out. "You may have to call the paramedics."

He took off running, walkie-talkie in hand, keys jangling from his belt and crepe-soled shoes squeaking across the freshly-shined lobby floor.

Gina and Bella turned to look at what was so alarming on the security monitor. There appeared to be a woman, floating on her back in the Jacuzzi, her legs splayed out on the decking. Had she fallen? Was she drowning? Was she dead?

When he arrived at the pool area, Derek was surprised to see a group of three men laughing and drinking, and no one seemed concerned about the woman who was hanging half in and half out of the hot tub.

He ran over to the hot tub. There was a tray with wine bottles and glasses teetering precariously at the edge of the whirlpool, next to the woman. Derek's first thought was that she had passed out from the combination of alcohol and the heat from the tub. Her face was above the water, her eyes were closed, and she was moaning. "Ma'am," he called out as he removed his shoes and belt and then he jumped into the hot tub next to her.

She was startled. "What the hell are you doing?" she yelled at him as he attempted to lift her out of the water. She yanked her arm away from him. "Leave me alone!"

"Ma'am, are you hurt?" He looked her over and noticed that her bikini bottoms were missing. "What happened? Did someone hurt you?"

"No! Let go of me! Can't a girl just get some peace and quiet?" She pulled herself up. "I was just . . ." she paused and chose her words carefully, "relaxing."

Apparently, she had strategically positioned her body to use the Jacuzzi jets to pleasure herself, a type of hands-free masturbation.

"Oh my god!" Bella shrilled. "That's Rose Marie de Bloc!"

Rose Marie was one of the newer residents of the top floor residential suites. She was the sauced widow of Hugh de Bloc, a hedge fund executive who had conveniently died from a heart-attack in the foyer of their Upper Manhattan home while the FBI were there arresting him for embezzlement. With Hugh dead, having never actually been trialed and found guilty, Rose Marie retained their fortune—for the time being, at least. Rose Marie's attorney, Saul Saltzman, advised her to keep a low profile, so she moved from New York City to San Francisco, hoping that the authorities would forget about the de Bloc debacle. She had loved her husband, their lifestyle, and everything that his money could buy. She never had any interest in cultivating hobbies or friends— unless plastic surgery and cocktailing were considered hobbies and rented post-facelift day nurses were her friends. Why should she? She had money and could buy hobbies and friends. Rose Marie used to say "Why should I bother with needlepointing a pillow, when I could stop on my way home from the hairdresser and buy one already done?"

But now, with very little tissue-paper-thin skin left to lift, pull, plump, or rearrange, she was unblinking, puckered, tight-faced, alone, and bored. Since moving to the hotel's residential floors she could regularly be found in the dark hotel bar drinking her dinner and flirting with male guests. Alcohol restored the years lost while she was married to Hugh. Vodka made her feel younger. Gin made her feel sexy and feisty. Olives, cocktail onions, and lemon twists, were salad. The dark lighting masked her creepy neck, aging hands, and Brillo-textured hair. When sitting at the bar of the Shipley Hotel, Rose Marie was young, fresh, and beautiful.

"Young man," she'd whisper to a young solo traveler, "You, yes you. You look lonely. Hey," she'd engage him, "I have a question for you. How old do you think I am?" Then she would turn her spinning barstool toward him and warn, "Now remember, it's not nice to insult a lady." When a polite gentleman played along, answering, "Oh, I don't know, thirty-nine? Forty?" She'd pounce, attempting to make him hers for the evening. "You don't have to pay the prices down here in the bar, when I have a full bar up in my apartment." Smiling her smeared lipstick smile, she'd then drop her key in front of him and walk toward the elevators.

"That's Rose Marie the Cougar!" Belle whispered in a voiceless holler.

"I thought you were drowning," Derek tried to explain as he stood soaked in the hot tub.

"Well, you thought wrong." She eyed him and changed her tone. "What's your name, handsome? I'm Rose Marie, but you can call me Rose or Rosie or pussycat." She seductively made a growling sound.

"I'm Derek. Let me help you up." He continued, "You can't be doing *that* in the Jacuzzi. It's against the rules."

"Says who, Derek, mister security man?" She pointed to the posted sign. "It says no running, no diving into the shallow end, and it says no horseplay. But it doesn't say anything about," she raised her penciled on eyebrow, "jillin' off . . . you know, pleasuring myself with the Jacuzzi jets."

He stood there speechless.

"Well, Derek," she purred as she stood up. "I wasn't drowning, but I can always use some mouth-to-mouth." She looked him up and down, then partially closed her drunken eyes, and allowed her tongue to slither out between her parted lips as she leaned in for a kiss.

Startled, Derek meant to take a step back but fell over into the water. Rose Marie's reaction was split second. With the reflexes of jungle cat, she pounced on him, wrapped her arms around him and kissed him, hard.

Bella and Gina stood with their eyes glued to the security monitor. This show was better than they could have imagined. Poor Derek; he was no match for Rose Marie the Cougar. "God, I wish we had some popcorn."

"I have ten bucks saying the Cougar gives Squeaky a blowjob." Bella reach in her pocket, pulled out a ten-dollar bill, unfolded it, and slapped it on the counter.

"Oh c'mon, Bella. Derek is a prude and takes his job way too seriously. Ten bucks says it won't happen." Gina slapped her ten on top of Bella's.

Without much more to do than watch a few of the Shipley's guests come through the lobby after one o'clock in the morning, Gina and Bella regularly placed bets on staff members; who was sleeping or screwing in the linen room, who was raiding the minibars in vacant rooms, or who was trolling for snacks in the kitchen. Occasionally, they would place bets on which guests were "hourly." That is, who was a paid escort or prostitute.

"Your clothes are soaked." Still a little inebriated, Rose Marie invited Derek to take a hot tub with her. "Since you're here and we're already wet . . ." she winked as she untied her bikini top. "Why don't we take advantage of the situation?"

Derek couldn't help himself; he was getting aroused. There was no way to hide it. His cheap, cotton trousers clung to him. "Oh, I don't . . ." He couldn't finish his sentence before she unzipped his pants.

"I think you deserve a reward for coming to my rescue." She reached into his pants.

Derek's mind was racing. He'd been told not to commingle with the hotel guests, but he couldn't help himself. The hours of a nighttime security guard are not complementary to a young man's social life. A young woman wants to be wined and dined, romanced under moonlight, not midday by a man in squeaky shoes. None of the women he was interested in would be willing to go on more than one lunch date or to a matinee. It had been two years since he took the job as a night security guard, two years since Derek had any physical contact with a woman. Two years since his high school girlfriend realized that Derek was not the man for her. She dumped him, hard.

He grabbed Rose Marie around her waist and hoisted her up onto the rough cement edge of the hot tub, opened her legs and proceeded to give her what she wanted: a proper and powerful screwing—one that she was unlikely to forget anytime soon, mostly due to the road rash she received from the rough cement decking.

"Oh! My! God!" Gina squealed. "I can't believe this!"

Bella turned around to look at the monitor, "Oh my God!" She repeated. "I think my eyes are going to start bleeding. Turn that off!"

"I can't!" Gina was pressing buttons and turning nobs but the monitor stayed on. "Brace yourself! This is something you won't be able to forget anytime soon." She sounded as desperate as the steersman of the Titanic when he tried at last minute to steer away from the iceberg.

"I've got it, Gina." Bella grabbed a laminated hotel amenities list and Scotch taped it over the monitor. "Disaster averted." They laughed.

Ten minutes later, Derek appeared soggy and squeaking across the lobby. "Sorry, Gus," he said to the floor man. "I didn't have a towel." As he passed the guest relations desk he mumbled "I'm going to the locker room to change my clothes. I fell in the pool."

"Okay, Romeo," Bella giggled, "we'll keep an eye on the security monitor for you."

Just then, Derek realized that his rendezvous with Rose Marie was caught on camera.

Bella looked up from her paperwork, still laughing to herself about the Jacuzzi scene when she noticed a young man, wearing a pajama top, gym shorts, and a pair of black socks as he walked quickly across the lobby toward the hotel shops. Within minutes he was back pacing the perimeter of the lobby, looking into each alcove and hallway.

"Excuse me, sir?" Bella called out. "May I help you with anything?"

"Yes, I hope so." He walked toward her. He seemed very anxious. "Is the gift shop open, or better yet, the dining room? I think I need a snack." He looked at his watch, "Oh no, huh? It's sort of late, isn't it?"

"Yes, sir," Bella came from around from the other side of the counter. She and the other staff members had been trained to detect signs identifying distraught guests and those suffering attacks associated with drugs, diabetes, or heart problems. "I think you should sit down. Shall I call a doctor for you?" She took his arm and led him to the lobby couch. "What is your name, sir?"

"Lipnick," he said, "I'm Franklin Lipnick." He sat down and calmed himself with a few deep breaths. "I'm sorry, miss. You're very nice, but I'm okay. I'm just anxious and I can't sleep." She offered a weak smile. "I swear there's nothing wrong with me."

"Phew," Bella sat down next to him. "If you're sure?" She blew out a sigh of relief. "Is there anything I can help you with?"

"I know it's silly, but I'd really like to talk," he looked around, "if you have a few minutes." His eyes were pleading.

"Sure," she looked around the empty lobby, "I have a few minutes." Bella lived for personal drama. Besides, Franklin Lipnick with his horn-rimmed glasses and his old-fashion waxed mustache was cute. She knew that she needed to keep her excitement in check. It was going to be difficult, but she knew it would be worth it. She extended her hand, "By the way, I'm Bella."

"Hi, Bella, it's nice to meet you." He gently shook her hand. "You see, Bella," he began, "I'm anxious because I'm meeting my father for the first time tomorrow." He raised his hand to his forehead. "I can't believe I said it out loud." He then explained that until his mother died a couple of months earlier, he didn't know who his father was. But while going through her papers he found his birth certificate identifying his father's name. "I really hope he's open to seeing me." He clarified, "Truthfully, I don't want anything from him. I think I'd just like to let him know that mom died and that I'm okay, and . . . " He looked like a little boy, "if he wants to get to know me, I'm open to it."

"Wow, Franklin, I'm sorry to hear about your mom." She flirted, "You seem pretty brave."

"I do have to admit, I didn't think I would be, but I'm very nervous to meet *him*." He looked around. "He's kind of famous."

"Wow, I could see that would be big deal." Bella nodded, "You're handling it better than I would," she confided. "I'd probably be drunk right about now. But," she was puzzled,

"Franklin, I hope you don't mind me asking but, why wouldn't he be open to seeing you? Doesn't he know you're here to meet him?"

"Oh yeah, there's this thing . . ." he stalled. "I'm not sure that he even knows I exist." Franklin knew he was risking being laughed at and turned away. After all, because his father was a celebrity, chances were that over the years people had come out of the woodwork claiming to be a relation. "When I tried to contact him, the closest I could get to him was his agent Norman Kravitz, and when I told him who my mother was, Norman remembered her fondly and set up this brunch meeting. He told me that my dad's health is failing and this news could be a shock. Mr. Kravitz suggested that it would best if I eased into telling him that I'm his son. But," he squared his shoulders, "I think I'll just go with what feels right."

"Yeah," Bella offered, "go with your gut. So," she asked, "why here at the Shipley? Does your dad live in San Francisco?"

"Well, yes." Franklin blurted, "I mean yes, he lives *here* . . . at the Shipley Hotel. Of course," he shook his head and laughed at himself. "You probably know him. Maybe you could tell me a little about him," he nodded and scooted forward. "His name is Oscar Pasternak."

2:00 A.M.

Maneuvering a full-sized rolling suitcase is difficult enough, but attempting to maneuver two of them—plus three shopping bags and an oversized Louise Vuitton shoulder satchel—through a relatively empty hotel lobby at 2:00 a.m. without being noticed is nearly impossible. It would be a challenge for even Penn and Teller. But Bunnie MacIntosh-Smith-Rothman felt she simply had no other choice. Her credit cards had been deactivated, her husband wasn't answering his cellphone, she didn't have a checkbook, and never carried cash. It was so gauche. She was known to say "Only poor people write checks, use coupons, and carry cash."

It was unfortunate timing. Bunnie not only had checked into the Shipley Hotel while some minor house construction was going on, but her hotel stay coincided with her husband Ed's bi-annual trip to New York to meet with his business manager. After reviewing Bunnie's credit card bills and itemized extravagances, which included destination-shopping sprees, daily trips to the department stores, and the waxing, buffing, and puffing of various body parts, Ed was disappointed. He had made himself clear. But still, Bunnie had shown little self-control when it came to spending his money.

"I should have known. She's just like my three ex-wives. I've told her dozens of times that I would not put up with any frivolous spending." Ed shook his head and said to Sidney, his business manager, "You know what to do. Cut off the cards. I'll deal with it and *her* when I get home."

Bunnie had only learned about her sudden lack of credit earlier in the day while trying to use her platinum card to pay for a new must-have and will-simply-die-if-I-don't-have handbag at the Coach store.

After attempting to process the sale, the store's sales associate discretely pulled Bunnie to the side and informed her of the problem. "Ma'am, do you have another card? There appears to be a problem with this one. It has been declined."

"That's impossible. *You* have clearly made a mistake." Bunnie exhaled with frustration as she unsnapped her wallet again. She handed the salesgirl a small pile of other Visa and American Express cards and told her to pick one, then suggested that the salesgirl was "some type of a moron" and should sign up for a vocational class to learn the most basic of salesclerk duties. "I shouldn't be mad at you," she said to the girl. "It's my fault, really. I mean, what do I expect?" She said loudly, "You're just a shop girl. I really need to lower my expectations of people."

As she attempted to process one after another, the sales girl silently cheered when each of Bunnie's credit cards were declined.

"Get your store manager!" Bunnie barked, "Such incompetence!" She slammed her well-manicured hand down on the counter. "I insist on speaking with the manager of the store, right this very instant!"

"I'm Ashley Morrell, the location manager." She walked Bunnie to a quiet place in the store. "Ma'am, I am so sorry. There appears to be an issue with all of the credit cards. We simply cannot process them. What I will do for you is hold your selections while you clear up this misunderstanding." Her smile was pitying. She had seen this scenario a hundred times before. "Please let me know if I can be of help in any way."

Bunnie pulled her cellphone out of her purse. First she speed-dialed her husband Ed. The call went directly to voice-mail. Then she pressed the preprogrammed "666" number. Sidney Feinstein, Ed's business manager, answered the phone. "Oh hello, Bunnie." He recognized the number on the caller ID function. "I've been meaning to call you. I met with Ed yesterday and he ordered that all credit and charge cards be put on hold. Ed wanted you to know that there is $500 cash in upper-right-hand desk drawer in the home office for inci-dentals until Sunday night when he gets home."

"But, I need . . ."

"Sorry, Bunnie" Sidney interrupted her, "this is what Ed asked me to tell you. I am not authorized to give you any-thing more at this point. You'll have to take it up with Ed on Sunday."

When the phone call with Sidney ended, Bunnie knew what was coming next. It wasn't so much a threat or a pattern as it was a promise. Ed constantly referred to the outrageous spending habits of his three previous wives and had made it clear that he would not put up with it from Bunnie. He would say, "I'll give you almost anything within reason, and I ask for very little in return. But if you take advantage of me, you're cut off. We're done."

She knew she was on borrowed time. After his three pre-vious marriages, love and devotion were no longer factors. For Ed, marriage was a business arrangement. Bunnie was not so much married as she was sponsored, much like a large corporation sponsors an athlete. As long as Bunnie continued to make a good showing, turn a blind eye to questionable dealings, avoid creating any negative press, and control her spending habits, she would remain Mrs. Rothman. But she had gotten carried away. She had lost track of the rules of the arrangement and now Bunnie either had to find a way to get back into her husband's good graces or pack her bags.

The day was a disaster. Without any new shopping bags, she felt naked. Thank goodness for her lunch pals Frieda, Olivia, Prima, and Nona. They called themselves the "Bitches Who Lunch." After hearing Bunnie's horrendous tale of woe about Ed's "overreaction" and him cutting off the credit cards because of a few shopping sprees, the "Bitches" were more than willing to pick up the tab for her two glasses of chardonnay, a popover and a seafood cobb salad at Niemann Marcus' Rotunda restaurant.

Bunnie's was not a cautionary tale. It was a very real reminder about the guaranteed fate of each member of the Bitches Who Lunch if they slipped up. Nona De Ventura offered, in solidarity, to boycott the Coach store for two full weeks. But that was about all she could offer. Though they were all comrades, sitting there sipping their twenty-five-dollar glasses of wine, the Bitches Who Lunch all knew this might be the last time they were all together. Bunnie had become the injured member of the herd. The rest of the Bitches would have to leave her behind and continue moving if they wanted to survive.

Bunnie knew what she needed to do. She had to locate and build a solid alliance, so she switched on her cellphone and dialed Felicia Monsaurat, who she regularly saw at her Pilates class. Felicia was a former member of Bitches Who Lunch and had somehow managed to land on her feet after the divorce from her husband, Pierre. The two made plans to meet that afternoon at the Four Seasons Hotel bar for cocktails. There was no time to waste.

"Felicia, what am I going to do? This came out of nowhere. I wasn't prepared this time." Bunnie squeezed a lime wedge over her vodka and tonic.

"Bunnie, honey, you need to buy some time." Felicia counted out the steps on her fingers. "Number one, you need to get an attorney and number one-A, you need to get to the safety deposit box. Can you do that?"

"Well, I think so. I was supposed to be at the Shipley Hotel for a few more days, but now that my credit cards have been cut off . . ."

"What? What are you doing? You're making his case for him. You need to get out of there. Like those tree-hugging nature nuts say, 'leave no trace.' Pack your bags and get out of there . . . tonight."

"Thank goodness for my girlfriends. Without your love and support, I'd starve." But she knew better; a more accurate statement would have been, "Without any money, I'd starve for friendship." Felicia understood. She paid for the cocktails.

Bunnie returned to the hotel frantic. She had been a guest at the hotel for the past four days, in a six-room, $3000 a night luxury suite. She had used room service and had also signed room charge tabs at the spa, the bar, and the boutique. She estimated that the bill had to be about $15,000. Felicia suggested that Bunnie should simply slip out of the hotel and then in a week or so, after Ed had a chance to calm down, he could pay the bill.

The more she thought about it the more indignant she became. *This is incredibly humiliating. How could Ed put me in this situation? This is his fault, after all. What did he expect? Romancing me and schtupping me with platinum cards and sky-high credit limits . . . then what? He strips them away like Lucy van Pelt pulls away Charlie Brown's football. What have I done? I've made that sagging, pasty, Viagra-popping, self-important troll of a man look good, that's what I've done. And this is the thanks I get?* Bunnie pouted as she packed her bags and planned her next move. She had no intention of standing at the front desk with the lowly hotel workers and explain the situation to *them*.

The bill would be taken care of in a week or so, and that was that. There was no need to make a federal case out of it.

At 2:00 a.m. the lobby was sprinkled with a few late night, early morning characters. The hotel staff was used to seeing guests returning from their evenings out, perhaps a couple who had enjoyed an evening at the theater, an inebriated bride after her bachelorette party, and people bidding each other pleasant dreams as they headed up to their rooms after a night cap in the bar. But it was rare to witness someone moving in the opposite direction . . . with luggage . . . making a beeline to the door . . . without explanation or making a key-drop at the desk. When that person is wearing enormous dark Jackie O. style sunglasses in the wee hours of the morning, it usually means one of three things: the person is a celebrity who is attempting to move about without being recognized; the person has been crying; or, there is something suspicious going on and Jackie Faux is skipping out on her bill.

"Excuse me, ma'am?" Gina asked from behind the desk. "Is everything alright?"

Bunnie waved her hand, but didn't look up and she picked up her pace as she neared the doors.

Gina nodded at Derek "Squeaky" Barnes who briskly walked through the lobby and stood between Bunnie and the exit doors.

"Young man, please move out of my way." She waved him off. "I need to leave."

Gina came up behind Bunnie. "You'll pardon me for saying so, but it is a little unusual for a guest to be leaving us at 2:00 a.m. Is everything alright? Can I be of assistance?"

"That is not necessary. My husband will take care of it."

Gina motioned to the other clerk to follow the next step in procedure, "That's fine, ma'am. I'm not sure we've processed your departure. What is your name, please? I'll make a note of it." Gina nodded at Bella who knew what to do.

"Rothman," Bunnie said arrogantly. She was hoping that if she put forth a bitchy attitude, the staff would leave her alone. "Listen, I need to leave. Call Mr. Rothman next week . . ."

After typing some information into the computer, Belle picked up the phone and dialed the night auditor. She waited while he checked the Rothman credit card and pre-authorization amounts. "I see," she said. "Thank you." She hung up the phone and jotted down some notes: *Bunnie Rothman, credit card #4410069582, declined. Current charges $14,355. Notifications: four.* Then she walked over to Gina and handed the slip of paper to her.

"Mrs. Rothman, according to our notes, over the past two days, our staff has left several voicemail messages on both your room phone and your cellphone to inform you that the pre-authorization on your credit card was declined. Haven't you received those messages?"

"No. I can't be bothered . . ."

"I understand. Mrs. Rothman, do you have another credit card that we should use? Or would you like to use the ATM, or make a bank transfer, or call a friend with a credit card?" She smiled kindly, "We can take care of this right now."

"No. I told you, I'm not going to pay the bill. My husband will take care of it next week." She rolled her eyes at the incompetence she perceived. "I don't have time for this. Listen, miss, I need a town car or a taxi." She looked for a doorman. No hotel staff was standing at the door on the curb. "Could *someone* get me a taxi?" She was impatient.

"Yes, well," she nodded at Bella and led Bunnie to the lobby seating area. "Please have a seat and I'll call one. It should be just a few minutes."

Five minutes later a pair of policemen walked into the lobby. "Ma'am, are you Bunnie Rothman?"

"Is there something wrong?"

"Yes, ma'am. It appears that you are leaving and," he looked at her luggage, "without paying your room bill."

"I told them that I just don't have the money right now. My husband is in New York and will address this when he gets home. Honestly," she stood up and looked at him with disgust, "as a city worker, I couldn't expect you to understand. But this is how things are done." She pushed past him.

He grabbed her arm. "Ma'am, are you aware that you could be charged with theft for refusing to pay or making arrangements to pay your hotel bill? It is a misdemeanor, ma'am."

She yanked her arm away from him. "I didn't refuse, I said I'll let my huband know, and he'll take care of it. Do I look like I'm the type of person who doesn't have any money? You," she pointed at the policeman, "have insulted me and," she pointed at Gina, "you have insulted me. Don't think I won't be calling the owner of this hotel to tell him how I have been treated." She picked up her purse and placed the strap on her shoulder, then grasped the handles of her shopping bags. "I'm leaving." She nodded toward her luggage. "Can someone please follow me out with my other bags?"

"Ma'am, I need to inform you that if you step out of the hotel, you will be arrested and charged with theft."

"If you arrest me, I will call my attorneys. I will sue this city. I will sue this hotel. And," she looked at the policeman's name badge, "I will sue you, Officer Randall. I will sue you so deep and hard that it will make a rectal exam feel like a butterfly kiss. So," she pushed him again. "Get out of my way."

Officer Randall shrugged then grabbed the handles of her rolling luggage and followed her out the front door. As she turned to take the suitcases from him, he grabbed her wrist and pulled it behind her back. "Give me your other hand, Mrs. Rothman."

She pulled and tugged. "Let go of me. What are you doing?"

"Mrs. Rothman, I told you that if you left the building you would be arrested. If you keep struggling, I will cite you for resisting arrest too, which will give you two misdemeanor offenses."

She was suddenly struck by the reality of what was happening and she tried to explain the economics of her situation. "Officer Randall, let me explain a few things to you. Number one, I am the wife of a very rich, very powerful man. I'm not trying to intimidate you. I am just telling you, *that's* what I *do*. I have made a career of being a wife to wealthy men. That's it, and I'm good at it. I know it doesn't sound very modern or liberated, but I have no other marketable skills. I don't need to. I don't use a computer, I can't parallel park, and as I'm sure as you can attest to, my people skills are marginal. I can throw a nice dinner party, I can make even the most unappealing men look mildly attractive, but that's about all. Number two," she tried to play on his sympathy, "if people like me get arrested, we become a cocktail party joke and we get divorced. I am Mr. Rothman's fourth wife, and he is my third husband. I have reached my quota. Unlike men, women do not become more distinguished-looking and desirable with age. Women just get old."

"If people like me get divorced, we can't afford Botox or an eyelift or professional salon appointments and we start looking our age. And if we start looking our age, we become unmarketable, gravel-voiced, wrinkled-faced divorcees who can't get a man, or a job because we never took the time to learn anything. And if we can't get a husband or a job we will need public assistance and end up cutting coupons and, Office Randall, we don't know how to use coupons."

"I'm sorry about that, Mrs. Rothman, but—"

Bunnie interrupted, "As we have established, if you're going to arrest me, I think it's safe to assume that I will no longer be *Mrs.* Rothman. So go ahead and call me Bunnie."

3:00 A.M.

With just the hum of the floor-polishing machine filling the lobby, Gina sipped a cup of coffee and entered the next day's visitor information into the computer. Her concentration was interrupted by a loud thud against the revolving doors. A group of young women fell against the glass as they arrived back at the hotel after what seemed to be an evening of over-celebration. Gina shook her head. Clearly the combination of uncomfortable strappy sandals, too many jello shots and colorfully-named drinks left them graceless.

After a number of tries and help from a passerby, they made it through the doors and into the lobby. The person who appeared to be the guest of honor was being held up by her armpits by two other ladies. She was dressed in a cocktail-stained T-shirt with the words "Da Bride" appliquéd on it. In one hand she held a decorated, oversized plastic cup and in the other she was holding one of her shoes. Her coat was tied around her waist, and her French twist hairstyle was now a disentangled mess under her plastic, bejeweled tiara with a sad, limp piece of tulle hanging off to the side. Her eye makeup was smudged and her breath was so bad that it could be seen.

Jennifer, the bossy maid of honor, was busily directing traffic. "Pull yourself together." She turned to the girls holding Lori "Da Bride" upright and ordered, "Don't let her fall. She can't have any bruises tomorrow."

"Ooh, I don't feel so well." The bride suddenly looked green.

"Lori, you'll be alright." Another one of the ladies in a "Da Bridesmaid" T-shirt laughed. "Just put your head between your knees . . ."

"I'm gonna be sick." Lori dropped her shoe and pushed the girls away then ran for the lobby ladies' room.

"We can't be surprised. Lori ruins every party." Jennifer laughed and shook her head at her co-bridesmaids. "Remember last year at Thanksgiving when she cried and locked herself in the bathroom? I convinced her she had to sit at the kiddie table because Robert's ex-girlfriend was coming and she was going to be seated next to him. Oh for fuck's sake, it was a joke." Then she added sarcastically, "Robert has sure gotten himself a party girl. Pfft."

"Yeah," another one said as she burped. "She's way too sensitive and nervous. Who wants to put up with that? I give it a year." They all laughed.

Yvonne walked into the lobby after paying for the taxi. She just shook her head in disbelief. "Jennifer, why did you encourage Lori to drink so much? You know she's nervous about tomorrow."

"I'm not her mother," Jennifer snapped back. "C'mon, girls," she said to other bridesmaids. "I'm ready to go to bed." She turned to Yvonne, "You'll get her up to her room, won't you?"

Exhausted, Yvonne sat down on the lobby sofa and waited. She looked at her watch. Although she had taken a nap following her own emotionally-motivated, cosmopolitan-pity-party earlier in the afternoon, Yvonne was worse for wear. How did she end up babysitting her stepsister?

She and Lori had never been very close. Maybe it was because there was a ten-year age difference. Maybe it was because Yvonne was bitter. Not only was Lori beautiful and smart and had a killer body, everything in her life always seemed to move along so smoothly and perfectly as if it were choreographed by Twyla Tharp, while Yvonne's seemed to be filled with clumsy, unending effort with only mild success. She begrudgingly came to San Francisco to attend the wedding, however she had never really intended to participate in the bachelorette party. When Lori called her room at five o'clock to confirm that Yvonne would attend, there was almost a pleading quality to her voice.

Now that Yvonne had a moment to think about it, something about Lori seemed off-kilter. She seemed sad—not the way a bride is expected to be the just one day before her wedding. Yvonne shook the thought out of her head. *What do I know, anyhow?* Maybe it was just wishful thinking on Yvonne's part.

She looked around. The lobby was quiet. Only the hum of the floor-polishing machine broke the calm. She took a deep breath and smiled to herself. This was the most peaceful moment she had had all day. Gus, the floor man, made eye contact with her. "Good evening, miss." Yvonne nodded at him then looked at her watch again. She needed to go to bed to rest up for the wedding, where she would have to field questions such as "why aren't you married?" and "where is your boyfriend?" She'd give Lori a few more minutes, then go into the ladies' room to check on her. Lori, she figured, had probably gotten herself all worked up into a drunken tizzy about *the wedding*, the two or three hours out of her life when it just had to be *perfection*. Sheesh!

Yvonne laughed to herself because she knew the truth, the one thing friends and family never tell the bride. The truth was that although each young bride thinks that *her* wedding is the social event of the season, the soirée to top all other events of the past that will set a very high bar for weddings of the future, it is, in fact, what guests consider an obligation. Furthermore, they wish that six weeks earlier, when they received the heavy-gauged, eggshell-colored calligraphed invitation that they had checked the "No, regretfully I will be unable to attend" box on the RSVP card. That's the secret. A party is only important to the hostess. No one cares about your centerpieces or the music you selected for your first dance. Not one guest is concerned about your guestbook attendant, the decision about hot or cold passed hors d'oeuvres, the comfort of your shoes, or the length of your train. What do they care about? Parking, and if there will be an open bar. In fact, not only do the bride's friends not care about any of the details of the wedding, they will gather while the new bride is on her honeymoon to have a debriefing, and judge and criticize the whole event from start to finish.

When Lori emerged from the restroom, she looked like she had been run over by a truck and dragged a couple of miles. She was pale and sweaty, hunched over, and moving in slow motion. She pulled the tiara out of her hair as she plopped down on the lobby couch next to Yvonne. "I don't know what I was thinking." She looked around. "Where are the girls?"

"Your friends went to bed," Yvonne shrugged.

Lori smiled sadly, "I guess you've figured out by now that they really aren't my friends."

"I'm confused, Lori. Aren't they your bridesmaids?"

"I don't really have any close friends." She exhaled. "Most women don't really like me. I don't really know why. Anyway, those girls, my bridesmaids," she rolled her eyes, "they're Robert's sisters and cousins. They, along with Robert's parents, really don't think I'm good enough for him, and they've made it clear." She added sarcastically, "A real confidence-booster, huh?"

She explained, "Since mom and dad don't have any money to contribute to the wedding and I am buried in student loans, Robert's parents are paying for the whole thing. They haven't really allowed me to participate in the planning. In fact," she laughed pathetically, "I've been told to 'show up and look pretty.' And that's a quote." She looked defeated. "I don't think I'm any more important than the floral arrangements. I'm just along for the ride. And let's face it. No one really enjoys being a guest at a wedding."

Yvonne smirked.

Truthfully, Lori would not have been surprised if she had learned that her future mother-in-law had booked the venue years ago, and coincidentally, she just happened to be the woman Robert was seeing as the date neared. His proposal seemed forced and it was less than romantic. But Lori loved him and forgave the lack of romance. The months that followed were filled with secretive meetings between Robert and his mother and Lori was provided details on a "need-to-know" basis. "You should be thrilled," Robert's mother Sharon would try to explain. "You don't need to spend your time doing things like tasting cakes, listening to bands, and picking linens. I know what Robert likes, so I'll do it." It all left Lori wondering what she was getting herself into.

"Don't say that, Lori. I am certain that you're more important than the floral arrangements. I think you're just nervous. Who wouldn't be? What does Robert say about all of this?"

Lori appreciated Yvonne's attempt at making her feel better. But Lori knew the truth. Queasy and vulnerable, Lori's defenses were low and she decided to confide in her stepsister. "It is true. I told Robert that I was unhappy and that I felt disrespected. But he told me that I needed to get with the program and it's just the way his mother is." She shrugged, "He did agree that it would be easier and more meaningful to elope . . ."

"So, why didn't you?"

"Well, I love Robert. I really do. But if I'm being perfectly honest, I'd have to admit he's a bit of a mama's boy and he was afraid to go against her wishes."

Yvonne started laughing. "This is so sad, Lori." The more she tried to halt her laughter, the more intense it became. Her eyes filled with tears and she was gasping for air. "I'm sorry," She laughed harder. "Really, Lori, I am." She snorted. She held up her finger. "Give me a minute. I'll stop, I will."

"Do you have a mental disorder? Because you certainly have an odd way of showing sympathy and support. I'm beginning to understand why we have never been close." Lori stood up, planning to walk away from Yvonne.

"Please, sit down." She patted the couch. "I'm not laughing *at* you Lori, really." She calmed herself. "I'm laughing at myself."

"Why?"

"It's jealousy—nothing more, nothing less." She shrugged, "For as long as I can remember I've been envious of how you float through life with such ease. And as long as *I'm* being honest, I've always been a little pissed off because you're so naturally pretty, and you're sweet, too." She sat back realizing what she had just admitted. "But what I realized today, while I was drowning my misery with vodka and cranberry concoctions, is that I've been jealous and sad and angry and ashamed because I wished I was more like you. And now . . . to put the cherry and whipped cream on top of it all, you have found someone who loves you, and you're getting married . . . and I'm not. To be honest with you, I almost didn't come to see you get married."

"Really?"

"Yes," Yvonne offered. "It never occurred to me that this whole wedding . . . could be an awful experience for you."

"Well, it has been." She tossed her tiara on the table in front of her. "As a matter of fact, I'm dreading it, rather than looking forward to it. I've even considered calling it off." She caught herself and put her hand across her mouth. "I can't believe I just said that out loud." Though she had been feeling uneasy about the wedding for months, Lori had never actually verbalized it. How ungrateful she must sound.

"You're unbelievable! What's the matter with you?" Yvonne just shook her head. "You have to know this is your fault."

"What? *My* fault? Are you kidding me? Are you *that* jealous?" Lori shook her head. "Do you have Tourette's? I swear you must be diagnosable. Who says these things?"

"Why are you letting other people call the shots and ruining your day? How could you let someone—anyone else—take the day, and this experience for you?" Yvonne scooted to the edge of the sofa and pointed at Lori. "You have to know you're setting a precedent for Robert and his family. From this point forward Lori, your opinion and your feelings won't matter. Don't you get it? If you can't even rate as the number one, most important person at your own wedding, what are the chances that anyone will ever listen to you again?"

Yvonne looked at Gina, behind the front desk. She and the other clerk and Squeaky looked down and away, acting like they had not been listening. Squeaky pretended to be adjusting the security monitor.

"Excuse me. Yes, you at the desk. I know you've been listening," Yvonne pointed at Gina who looked around. "There's nothing else going on here. I'd be listening if I were you." She waved them over. "Do you have a minute? Would you come over here to help us out?"

Gina smiled and nudged Squeaky and Bella, "C'mon." They came around through the door and sat down with Lori and Yvonne.

"Here's the situation," Yvonne began. "This is Lori and she is supposed to be getting married tomorrow. Now, I'm not saying whether she should or shouldn't go through with it," She looked knowingly at Lori and placed her hand on Lori's arm. "I'm just looking for an opinion."

Squeaky looked at Gina and smiled. "Gina is known for her opinions." He laughed. "She has one for every situation."

"Okay, great. So here it is in a nutshell. Lori has been dating Robert for two years. He doesn't put her first. He doesn't defend her when his mother and family ignore her wishes. And tomorrow, it appears that she will be a guest at her own wedding. So," Yvonne got to the point, "I'm taking a poll. If you were disregarded and left out of the planning of your own wedding and your fiancé was afraid of his mother, would you go ahead with the wedding?"

"I don't know you, Lori—it's Lori, right?" Gina offered. "But this isn't just one day, it's the beginning of your life with this man," she rolled her eyes, ". . . and his overbearing mother. Trust me, I know. I think that if it were up to my mother-in-law and it was legal, she herself would be married to her son, my husband. You need to know you have what it takes to put up with that long-term." She winked at Bella, "Or, figure out where to hide your empty booze bottles."

Derek stood and listened quietly. When Gina finished, he spoke up. "Have you told Robert what *your* expectations are? I mean, have you spoken to him about what type of husband you expect *him* to be? Maybe he doesn't know. Some guys don't get it. It seems to me, he doesn't know what to do. He has made it clear to you that he's afraid of his mother, and you haven't said anything, so he assumes that you are perfectly fine to join him in the backseat of the family's drama car."

"No, I haven't told him." Lori looked down at her hands, "I guess I should." Lori realized that Yvonne was right. She had created the problem for herself. Having never spoken up, she let Robert and his mother dictate the terms of their relationship.

"I think you need to call him right now and ask him to come down here to the lobby." Derek explained, "Take his hands in yours and just tell him what you want. Clear this up before you put on your dress tomorrow. You owe it to him, and to yourself. It wouldn't be fair if you spent your entire marriage being resentful."

Gina realized that her mouth was wide open. Squeaky really amazed her.

"You know what?" Bella whispered to Gina. "Derek's kind of cute."

4:00 A.M.

Hal pounded on the passenger door. "Come on, Betty, get out of the truck and help me. It's four o'clock already, and we have tons to do today."

"Fine." Benny climbed down from the truck. "But if I look like hell, that's your fault. Slave driver."

Hal unlatched the lever and eased up the rolling door in the back of the truck, and Ben climbed in ready to unload the flowers. "Benny," Hal pointed to a carefully-constructed arrangement, "would you please hand that to me?"

The bouquet was stunning. It was composed of pink roses, blush peonies, tulips, paperwhites, gloriosas, lilacs, hyacinths, and ranunculus. The tall, rectangular vase was wrapped in a banana leaf. It may have been the most beautiful arrangement Hal had ever created. He smiled. He had been inspired. Like the flowers he chose, his evening with Pamela, just hours earlier, was delightful and fresh.

It had been years since he had been on a date. Their conversation was fluid and hours passed as they sipped wine at an outdoor table by the bay. They talked about art and music and the city and the beauty of the lobby at the Shipley Hotel. He smiled to himself, looking forward to the next time he would spend time with Pamela. Benny was so pleased to see his father smitten.

"Oh Romeo, Romeo, wherefore art thou . . . ?" Benny teased his father. "Are you ready?"

"You go ahead and start unloading the truck." Hal inhaled the smell of the arrangement. "I need to go and deliver this to the boutique."

Before Hal walked through the door and into the lobby, Ben ran from the truck and handed him a pen and a piece of paper. "Here," Ben stepped in front of his father and offered his back as a writing table. "Don't forget a note."